He took her empty champagne glass away and held it a moment, touching the warmth where her fingers had been. . . .

His gaze turned irresistible as he studied her, his smile sexy. "Forgive me, Princess, but you look good enough to eat . . . and I'm feeling a little like the big bad wolf tonight."

Edwina tried to return his smile but her heart was too erratic. There was no escaping him.

He tilted her chin up. "Your eyes changed when I said that. They darkened. Do you like it when I talk to you that way?"

Like it? Edwina felt a deep clutch of excitement that left her flushed and breathless. It wasn't a question that required an answer, luckily, because she couldn't have managed one if it had. Her body was having trouble remembering elemental things like breathing.

"Do you want to stay for the next act?" he asked.

She must have answered, because he took her hand and in a headlong rush led her to a waiting limousine. . . .

WHAT ARE *LOVESWEPT* ROMANCES?

They are stories of true romance and touching emotion. We believe those two very important ingredients are constants in our highly sensual and very believable stories in the *LOVESWEPT* line. Our goal is to give you, the reader, stories of consistently high quality that may sometimes make you laugh, sometimes make you cry, but are always fresh and creative and contain many delightful surprises within their pages.

Most romance fans read an enormous number of books. Those they truly love, they keep. Others may be traded with friends and soon forgotten. We hope that each *LOVESWEPT* romance will be a treasure—a "keeper." We will always try to publish

LOVE STORIES YOU'LL NEVER FORGET
BY AUTHORS YOU'LL ALWAYS REMEMBER

The Editors

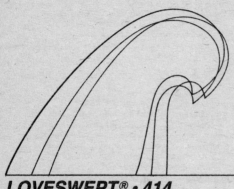

LOVESWEPT® • 414

Suzanne Forster
The Devil and Ms. Moody

BANTAM BOOKS
NEW YORK • TORONTO • LONDON • SYDNEY • AUCKLAND

THE DEVIL AND MS. MOODY

A Bantam Book / August 1990

LOVESWEPT® and the wave device are registered
trademarks of Bantam Books, a division of
Bantam Doubleday Dell Publishing Group, Inc.
Registered in U.S. Patent
and Trademark Office and elsewhere.

*If you would be interested in receiving protective vinyl
covers for your Loveswept books, please write to this address
for information:*

Loveswept
Bantam Books
P.O. Box 985
Hicksville, NY 11802

ISBN 0-553-44040-3

Published simultaneously in the United States and Canada

Bantam Books are published by Bantam Books, a division
of Bantam Doubleday Dell Publishing Group, Inc. Its trademark, consisting of the words "Bantam Books" and the
portrayal of a rooster, is Registered in U.S. Patent and
Trademark Office and in other countries. Marca Registrada.
Bantam Books, 666 Fifth Avenue, New York, New York 10103.

PRINTED IN THE UNITED STATES OF AMERICA

OPM   0 9 8 7 6 5 4 3 2 1

Prologue

The mountain was waiting for something.

High on a hilltop above Carbon Canyon Road a lone figure eclipsed the fiery corona of the falling sun. Powerfully built, seated astride an equally powerful machine, the man watched the sinuous road below. And waited with the mountain.

The motorcycle purred softly beneath him. His windswept hair flowed down his back, a symbol of strength, mastery, even savagery in ancient times. In another era the gleaming black beast between his legs might have been a stallion.

He was a loner, new to the area, but those who'd met him called him Diablo. Perhaps because of the name emblazoned in flames on his Harley Davidson motorcycle. More likely it was the reputation he brought with him—fearless, dangerous, a street fighter. A man who rode like the devil himself.

A rolling, thunderous sound caught the man's attention. He scanned the distance, alerted as the thunder split and a pack of motorcyclists swept around a curve in the road. Streaming through the canyon like an invading army, the pack slowed as one, rolled off the highway, and glided to a stop in front of a weathered wooden structure called Blackie's Bar.

Some thirty strong, the men wore jackets with the head of Zeus emblazoned on the back. The women, a few of them exceptionally beautiful, wore the same crest on their T-shirts and tank tops. The man watched the group disappear through the swinging doors of the saloon. Out to raise some hell, he thought. The Warlords were good at that. But what else went on in the back rooms of Blackie's Bar? Drug dealing? Smuggling? Soon he would know.

Again he reviewed his plan to gain membership into the secretive gang. Over the past weeks he'd passed every test they'd thrown at him, met every challenge. He'd won their grudging respect and met every requirement but one. The Warlords had surprisingly strong sanctions regarding women, and rogue males weren't allowed in the pack.

He twisted the throttle and sent a charge of energy through the beast's belly. It roared and trembled beneath him, impatient to be set free. The man was impatient too. He was ready, primed to make his move, to challenge for membership. Now all he needed was a woman.

"A motorcycle gang? Have you misplaced your alleged mind, Edwina Jean?"

Edwina Moody jotted the last entry on her "Things to Do" checklist, dropped her pencil in its holder along with a dozen others, all sharpened to a needle point, and sat back and looked at her younger sister.

Beth Moody was popping her grape bubblegum and pacing Edwina's bedroom loft with all the sixteen-year-old intensity she usually reserved for shopping malls.

"I don't plan to join the gang, Beth," Edwina said calmly. "Once I've found this Christopher Holt person and informed him that he's inherited a small fortune, my job is done."

Beth did her imitation of a punctured tire.

"Sheeeeeshhhh, Edwina." Shaking her head she fell back on Edwina's bed, arms flung out, then rebounded back up to her elbows. "So you're off to the wilds of California to find some weirdo who's joined a biker gang? Why in the world did you accept an assignment like that?"

"Call me crazy, Beth, but I like regular meals and a roof over my head." Edwina opened the top drawer of the same white-pine desk she'd done her high school homework on and lifted a stack of bills.

"Dad's debts—I'm still paying them off. And then there's *this*." Her voice dropped to a whisper as she picked up a legal document and ticked it ominously.

"The tax lien," Beth said, her voice hushing too. "Did you tell Mom yet?"

"Tell her what? That if I can't come up with fifty thousand by the end of the month, we're going to lose the house?" Edwina's throat closed on the last word, and when she tried to shrug away the sudden emotion, she couldn't.

"I *hate* men. I really do," Beth said, suddenly bitter. She rolled over and buried her face in one of Edwina's ruffled-chintz pillows.

Don't we all, Edwina thought, privately sharing Beth's enmity. It was hard to respect a man who would abandon his wife and two daughters and his failing business, all in one fell swoop. Their father, Donald Moody, simply hadn't come home from work one evening. He'd confessed his business losses and his extramarital affair in a letter postmarked Bora Bora that arrived two weeks later, postage due.

Katherine, Edwina's mother, collapsed. Beth went into a panic about what her friends would think, and Edwina took charge. Refusing to file bankruptcy, she left college, sold the hardware business, and took a job as a field researcher for an agency that located missing heirs. Now, a year later, she'd barely made a dent in the mountain of debts, and the IRS had slapped a tax lien on their modest Norwalk, Connecticut, house.

It had been a hellish year for the Moody women, but Edwina was strong, and Beth was young and resilient. It was Katherine that Edwina worried about. She knew her mother would never recover from the shock of losing her home.

"I have to go, Sis. If I can find Holt, my percentage of the estate should more than cover the lien."

Beth moaned into the pillow.

Edwina walked to her sister's half-buried head and ruffled the blond curls, still baby-fine and a shade or two lighter than her own. "You stay here and hold down the fort, Bethany. Take care of Mom for me, okay?"

One

"That's it, lady. Blackie's Bar. I hope you've got some brass knuckles with you."

Edwina dug through her purse for the fare and deposited the bills in the taxi driver's outstretched palm. "Wait for me, will you please?" she said. "I shouldn't be long."

Letting herself out of the cab, she shaded her eyes against the relentless late-summer sun as she faced the ramshackle bar. Except for the explosive laughter and throbbing jukebox music that blasted through the saloon doors, it might have been just another isolated tavern stuck away in southern California's San Gabriel Mountains. The old building seemed to quake with every decibel.

Blackie's. The biker bar was everything Edwina feared it would be and a few things she couldn't have even imagined. She'd done her research, but perhaps nothing could have prepared her for the ten-deep rows of gleaming choppers that jammed the gravel parking lot, most of them with more chrome than a gourmet restaurant's kitchen. Connecticut wasn't known for its motorcycle gangs.

Edwina approached the closest machine and perused the artwork on the shiny black tank. A death's-head grinned at her above the blood-red words Hell on Wheels. Wicked-looking thing, Edwina thought, shuddering.

"You sure you want to go in there, lady?"

Edwina was sure of only one thing at that moment. She wanted to be on a jet back to Norwalk. However . . . She brushed wisps of damp hair from her forehead and reminded herself that confidence started with correct posture. However, her research indicated that Blackie's was a bikers' mecca, the place to be if you preferred two wheels to four. She'd been tipped that everyone showed up there eventually, and she was counting on that to be true. Especially since Holt had last been spotted riding with a San Gabriel motorcycle club called the Warlords who were known to hang out at Blackie's.

"I'm sure," she told the driver with a leveling glance at his grimace of disbelief. Like Beth, he obviously thought she was a mental case. "You will wait?" she repeated, relieved when he shrugged a yes of sorts. Wetting her dry lips, she hitched her purse strap over her shoulder and started for the swinging doors of Blackie's Bar.

If Edwina Moody was "mental," as some people obviously thought, she was also a woman of unusual fortitude. It had taken all her powers of reason and persuasion to talk her boss, Ned Dillinger, into giving her the Holt case. She'd been selected over more experienced and better qualified investigators, primarily because Ned respected the way she'd fought for the assignment. She'd come to him already having done an enormous amount of research on Holt's family background. Ned liked that kind of initiative. He also understood that it wasn't just ambition that was driving Edwina. It was also her family predicament.

What Ned didn't know about Edwina, however, was what that predicament had cost her in her own career goals. She'd set aside her graduate project, an innovative plan to combine day-care programs for preschoolers and the elderly. Her work as a nurse's aide before she'd entered college had convinced Edwina that too many senior citizens languished in convalescent-care facilities with nothing to stimulate their minds and hearts.

It was an issue that wrenched at her own heart, and leaving school had been a difficult decision. However, family came first. Of all the ties that bind, Edwina believed most strongly in responsibility to one's kin. In fact, having relinquished her dream in favor of salvaging her family, she was all the more committed to finding Christopher Holt. Even if it meant bearding the wild ones in their den.

A jeering chorus of whistles and catcalls assaulted Edwina as she pushed through the bar's entrance. Bewildered, she stopped to orient herself before she realized the uproar wasn't meant for her. As her senses adjusted to the noise and the darkness, she became aware of the musky scent of perspiration and laboring muscles. It overrode everything else, even the odor of stale beer.

"Take him out, Mad Dawg!" someone shouted. "You can do it!"

Edwina could discern customers seated at the bar and in booths, but the real action was in the room's center. A rowdy knot of bikers was gathered around an arm-wrestling match in full swing. Luckily no one seemed to have the slightest interest in Edwina Jean Moody with her dishwater-blond ponytail, patch-pocket cardigan, and sensible penny loafers. She'd intentionally preserved her "Connecticut" look on the chance that Holt might befriend or otherwise respond to someone from his former world.

Edwina approached the arm-wrestling contest quietly, drawn by the spectacle. She'd never gone in for spectator sports, and yet the display of raw physical aggression, and even rawer language, was strangely riveting.

The two wrestlers, sheened in sweat, were locked in mortal combat. They seemed to be closely matched in physical strength, and yet one of them was clearly the superior wrestler. Edwina found herself staring, both fascinated and repelled as she took in every detail.

The pro was a ruddy man with a red-tinged beard and a silver earring piercing his nose. But it was the other man, the challenger, who riveted Edwina's attention. He had a stallion's mane of long dark hair and the most unusual green eyes she'd ever seen. They looked nearly transparent but were infused with an energy bright enough to make her want to shade her own eyes, even in the murky bar.

"Ah, sí, . . . el Diablo," a woman breathed near Edwina's shoulder.

Edwina glanced behind her and saw one of the barmaids, a slender Hispanic woman, coveting the green-eyed wrestler with what could only be called admiration. Naked admiration.

Edwina glanced at the man again, at his clenched jaw and the sweaty magnificence of his straining male flesh. His fight to keep his arm from being pinned was almost painful to watch. His muscles bulged with the massive effort, and his veins were ridged like cables. And yet, even in apparent defeat, he gave off more power, heat, and concentrated killer instinct than Edwina had ever witnessed in her life, firsthand or otherwise.

A buzz of surprise went up as he gave a violent cry. His face twisted with gut strength as he stopped the brutal onslaught inches from the tabletop. For several seconds he was frozen in agony, and then he began to turn the contest around. It was excruciating to watch, but Edwina couldn't turn away. The wrestler let out another savage sound and redoubled his efforts. Inch by racking inch, he forced the bearded man's arm upward until he had the crowd whistling and screaming.

Edwina's heart went crazy at that point, and she turned away from the scene with one thought on her mind. Who would ever have believed such primitive male behavior could be so . . . several words came to mind, but the only one that stuck was fascinating. *Fascinating?*

The crowd's roar nearly took the roof off.

"Sí! Diablo! Sí!" the barmaid shouted.

Edwina realized that he must have won, but she wouldn't let herself turn around. The scene had been too raw and disturbing. Her neck muscles were taut, her temples damp just from watching. She dug into the zipper pocket of her purse and pulled out a dog-eared picture of a painfully thin, freckle-faced teenager with limbs too long for his torso and a harmonica clutched in his hand. Christopher Holt at fourteen. Enough with the arm wrestling, she told herself. Holt was the reason she was here.

Edwina frowned at the picture in her hand. It wasn't going to be easy tracking down a thirty-four-year-old man with a picture taken twenty years ago. Her only other description of Holt had come from the California DMV. They'd tightened their disclosure regulations, but she'd used her agency's law-enforcement connections to obtain his vital statistics. He'd been twenty when he applied for the license, just under six feet tall and 140 pounds, with brown hair and hazel eyes.

Holt's case was one of the strangest Edwina had ever worked on. He'd dropped out of Harvard at the age of nineteen. He'd moved out of his uncle's Connecticut estate for unknown reasons. And then he'd virtually disappeared for fifteen years.

Using the man's sporadic credit and employment history, Edwina had tracked him through a series of odd jobs in the southern California area, but she had only the picture and the DMV stats to identify him. When she complained to the estate's attorneys about the photograph's age, she learned it was the only one they'd been able to locate.

The bartender was drawing a mug of draft beer as Edwina approached. She slid onto a barstool and positioned the photograph in a stream of light from the door. "Ever seen this guy?" she asked.

The bartender squinted at it and went back to his beer. "Try the skateboard park," he said, propelling the full mug down the counter past Edwina.

"Please," she said. "It's important."

"*Puleeeze?*" The question, which came from behind Edwina, was followed by raucous laughter. "Now that's what I like—a woman who asks nice!"

Edwina spun around and stared dead-level into the beard of the sweaty red-headed arm wrestler.

He snatched the picture out of her hand and eyeballed it. "What do you want with boys, baby? When you could have a man."

The crowd whooped and catcalled. "A whole lot of man!" someone yelled.

Suddenly Edwina was the main attraction. Surrounded by leering bikers and feeling very much like the last fudge brownie at a bake sale, she scanned the room, searching for a way out. When she realized that she didn't have a prayer, she decided to make the best of the situation. She rescued the photo from the bearded man's hand and held it up.

"As long as we're gathered here," she said, pressing against the bar and forcing a smile, "I wonder if any of you might tell me whether you've ever seen this person before?"

"Get a load of that pencil-neck geek!" someone guffawed.

A roar went up, punctuated by howls of "Hey, baby, you can play *my* harmonica!" and "Wanna see my freckles?"

Edwina clearly wasn't going to get the cooperation she'd hoped for. "Well, thank you anyway," she said, sliding along the bar as she inched her way toward the door. "I'll just try the restaurant down the road."

She spotted daylight through a crack between two pairs of huge shoulders and started for it, only to find herself snagged by the wrist and jerked back.

"Aw, shucks, honey, not so fast." The bearded man dragged her into his arms like a rag doll and planted a wet, bristly kiss on her dodging features.

Edwina ducked and shoved with all her might. Thankful for her self-defense training, she landed a sharp kick to his shinbone, then twisted violently, pulling partially free. She swung back around, thinking to jam an elbow in his ribs when the man was ripped bodily from the very floor he stood on.

Rocked back on her heels, Edwina fought to catch her balance. When she looked up, her assailant was dangling in the grip of the green-eyed wrestler, who seemed about ready to plant a kiss or two of the roundhouse variety.

"Put me the hell down," the bearded man snarled.

The green-eyed man spoke softly, almost inaudibly, his voice no more than a hair-raising whisper. "I won our match, Mad Dog, and I'm claiming my prize. I want the woman."

"That ain't f-fa-fair," Mad Dog stuttered wildly as his captor shook him like a troublesome puppy. "Aw, take her then," he bellowed. "Crazy broad. I don't want her anyway."

There was a momentary scuffle as Mad Dog hit the floor. The two men went head-to-head, and then, apparently thinking the better of it, Mad Dog swore a blue streak and stomped off.

Edwina was weak with relief. "Thank y—" She lost the words as she met her rescuer's gaze. A corona of hoarfrost ringed his brilliant green irises, but beneath the glacial ice, his eyes were ablaze. It was angry fire. Consuming fire. The kind that had burned witches in Salem. For a second, Edwina wasn't sure if she'd been saved or condemned to a fate more horrible than Mad Dog.

"Let's get out of here," he said, gripping her arm and hauling her with him toward the door.

Edwina was in no position to argue. Nor did she attempt to. As she stumbled to keep up with him she realized that she would be wise to save her strength in case he had to fight him off too.

It wasn't until he had her outside and on the periphery of the parking lot that he pulled her around to face him. "What is this, Princess? A sorority dare? You lose a bet or something? You uptown babes got a weird way of getting your kicks."

He held her back and looked her over, his eyes loitering on the heaving motion of her breasts and the front zipper of her gabardine slacks. It was a long illicit look that was meant to strip her naked, in every possible sense of the word. And it did so, very effectively.

If Edwina bridled under his crude inspection, she also felt a tight, painful thrill. And hated herself for it. *Babes*. That word had just made her top-ten list of most-hated male epithets.

He breathed the next words, his voice never rising above the hair-raising whisper she'd heard in the bar. "Those are big bad wolves in there, Princess. They eat baby chicks like you for breakfast—every day of the week."

"Thanks for your concern," Edwina said stiffly. "Now if you'll please let me go."

Amazingly, he did. Stepping back, he left her to reorganize herself hastily, and as she did, he drew the crumpled photograph from her grip.

"What do you want with this guy?" he asked.

"Why?" She tucked her blouse into her slacks and shook her clothing into place. "Do you know him?"

"I ask the questions."

Now that she had some distance from him, Edwina allowed herself to check out the man who'd hauled her out of Blackie's. His features were hard-edged and handsome, almost too handsome for the sort of reckless life he undoubtedly lived. Harsh angles and an obviously predatory nature kept him from being pretty. *Shadowed, sensual, feral.* Those were the words that described his look. Not pretty. *Never* pretty.

He was a taller than her by a half a foot at least, densely muscled, and indecently broad-shouldered. His black leather vest gleamed against suntanned skin, and the unlaced opening revealed a dark diamond of chest hair . . . Her eyes flicked away as the awareness sank in that he was bare-chested under the vest.

"What's his name?" he said, as though he'd asked the question several times while she was ogling him. "And what do you want with him?"

"Holt—his name is Holt. And I'm not at liberty to tell you what I want with him. That's for his ears only, but it is urgent that I find him."

"Urgent?" He flicked the photograph with his fingers and then slid it into the breastpocket of Edwina's blouse, his fingers burning through the silky material. His eyelashes flickered, and a smoky smile emerged as he watched her cheeks go hot. "I'll tell you what's urgent, Princess—"

Edwina's heart pounded wildly under the pressure of his hand. It felt as though he were actually touching her, as though there were no fabric separating their skin. His voice was low, rusty, intimate.

"It's urgent that you hightail it out of here."

Withdrawing his fingers slowly, he gathered a handful of her blouse into his fist and drew her to him. "Before you get yourself into trouble."

Edwina nearly drowned in the saturating green of his eyes. The scent of him was hot and bewildering. It was musky body heat and the tart pungency of draft beer. It was sweat-softened leather and something else that she knew instinctively was sexual. He gave off the scent of male sexuality the way a lightning bug gave off sparks.

"Yes, maybe I should go then."

Even if Edwina had wanted to move, she couldn't have. Not right then. He was too close, too intimately paralyzing to her thought processes. She could feel his fingers curled against the flesh of her left breast and his leg pressed against an intimate part of her body. His thigh was nudging the inner curve of her hipbone in a shockingly familiar way.

But the oddest thing was that she had no desire to move. The solid heat of him felt unexpectedly riveting, and the way he was staring at her, with a kind of dawning male curiosity, as though he'd just discovered something about her he couldn't readily dismiss . . . well, it made her feel alive in a way that she couldn't begin to rationalize.

"What are you staring at?" she asked.

"I'm trying to figure out what a woman like you is doing at a dive like this."

Looking for a biker, of course. That was her thought, but the words that came out were "A woman like me?"

By this time Edwina had begun to have glimmers of feelings that she could hardly believe. A pulse was ticking in her throat, and her nerves were responding to the pressure of his thigh with quick little sparks of energy. It wasn't that she actually *liked* the way this roughneck was touching her, and yet . . . *something* was happening.

"You're not a cop," he said, "or a private eye. I can spot either, blindfolded. No, you're too prim and preppie for that. And yet you did a pretty fair job of defending yourself in there."

He continued to inspect her, and Edwina continued to permit it, aware that her breath was suspended in her throat. She was also aware that some rational part of her mind had stepped back and was watching this whole episode with interest. Edwina Moody mesmerized by a black-leather biker?

He touched her chin, and Edwina tilted it up automatically, curious about what he was going to do next.

"I can't figure you, Princess," he said finally, his voice lowering again to a sexy dream of a whisper. "You're kind of cute when you're not bashing heads."

His eyes drifted to her lips, and Edwina felt a thrill she couldn't have denied in a million years.

"Yeah, cute . . . that's a sweet mouth," he said.

"It is?" For all her rational detachment, Edwina found his observation absolutely fascinating. A "sweet" mouth. No one had ever said such a thing about her before. A dutiful daughter, a good student, an efficient worker, but never a "sweet" anything.

Curious, she drew a finger along her lips and felt their satiny texture. My goodness, she thought, was that how her mouth would feel to a man? To him?

"What the hell are you doing?"

His eyes darkened as he watched her touch herself, and Edwina felt a sharp thrill of anticipation. It wasn't immediately apparent to her what she'd done to elicit such a response, but she did know that her breath was rushing the way it had in high school when Skipper Henderson had followed her into the girls' locker room.

It hit her all at once that she wanted this man to press her up against the shower wall and kiss her, just the way she'd wanted Skipper Henderson to in tenth grade. The notion shocked her now almost as much as it had then, but the urgency of it wouldn't be denied. Nervespun sensations sparkled inside her. She had wanted to taste Skipper Henderson's warm, sweet breath. She had wanted his mouth against hers and his hands all over her body. And she wanted that again. *Now, here, with this man.*

A sound slipped from Edwina's throat, startling her. A shudder moved through her limbs. What was she doing? This was crazy, utterly *nuts*. This man wasn't a varsity football star! He was an arrogant roughneck she wouldn't haven't spoken two words to back home in Connecticut, and here she was, vividly imagining how he was going to follow her into a shower stall and make love to her!

He bent as though to kiss her, and Edwina gasped in alarm, pushing him away. "This isn't the girls' locker room, mister. And you're no Skipper Henderson."

"Skipper who?" His brows flattened as he let the bunched silk of her blouse slip from his fist. "What kind of a weird broad are you?"

Edwina clutched at the neckline of her blouse. *Babe. Broad.* His grasp of the language was appallingly limited.

"You were right the first time," she said. "I have to be going." Twisting free from his grip, she started back toward Blackie's. And counted herself very lucky. The close calls were stacking up in this case. She *was* free, however, she reminded herself. And if she was off to an unfortunate start with the investigation, at least she could give herself a point or two for survival skills.

That was when she realized her taxi was gone. *Gone!* She hesitated, aware that her options were frighteningly limited. She either found a phone or she walked. With a quick glance at the green-eyed biker, who was observing her with dark curiosity, she ruled him out as an option and headed for Blackie's. The bartender must have a phone behind the counter. If she could slip in just long enough to ask him to call her a taxi . . .

A faint smile softened the biker's features as he followed Edwina's progress with his eyes. He kind of liked the way she walked, although he wasn't sure why. There was nothing sexy about it, but she moved with purpose, and her ponytail bounced with every step. He had a hunch she did just about everything with purpose, and the ramifications of that thought intrigued him. It was where she was headed that disturbed him.

"You got a death wish, lady?" he called after her. "Where the hell are you going?"

"To call a taxi." She tossed the words over her shoulder and kept walking. "I don't see any pay phones around here. Do you?"

"A taxi? You came here in a taxi?" Purpose, hell. She was either gutsy or crazy, and he was betting on both, a dangerous combination. He caught up with her in a few easy strides. "You go back in that bar, you're on your own. I'm not riding to the rescue again."

She ignored him, and in the same instant that he decided he liked her spirit, he also saw the perfect way to get her attention. He caught hold of her blond ponytail, gave it a quick tug, and stopped her cold. She let out an incredulous squeak and snapped her head to free herself. When he didn't let go, she whirled, and with a flashing right hook that apparently startled even her, she swung at him.

He caught her small fist much as a catcher would

a pop fly. "Watch where you put that thing," he said, grinning. "You could hurt somebody."

"What are you? A cave dweller? Java man?"

"I saved your life, and this is how you thank me?"

Edwina was more astonished than angry, but his soft snort of laughter made it all the more difficult to settle herself down. "Fine," she said, "if you won't let me call a taxi, how do you suggest I get back to my hotel? *Walk*?"

He scratched his sandpapery jaw thoughtfully, then strode to a black beast of a motorcycle and knocked back the kickstand with his boot. It was the same bike she'd inspected before, complete with the grinning skull and Hell-on-Wheels logo.

"Hop on," he said. "I'll take you."

Edwina stared at him in disbelief. He actually thought she was going to get on that fire-breathing dragon with him at the controls? "No, thank you," she said emphatically. "I think I will walk."

She started for the road with every intention of walking until she hit the Pacific Ocean—or the nearest pay phone—whichever came first.

Two

"Ten miles to the nearest phone," he said as Edwina brushed past him. "Maybe more."

"I can use the exercise." Feeling his eyes on her backside, she tugged her lamb's-wool cardigan down and continued walking.

He seemed content just to watch as she started off down the road, so content in fact that she wondered if she was heading in the wrong direction. Surely he wouldn't let her wander off and get hopelessly lost in these mountains?

A couple of cars passed her as she began her trek down the mountainside, and she made up her mind that she would flag down the next one and ask directions. The August sun was meltingly hot, and she wasn't dressed for warm weather. At least she'd worn good walking shoes.

She must have covered close to a mile by the time she heard the drone of another engine behind her. Her forehead was dripping, and her calf muscles were on fire. She turned to wave and saw flying dark hair and an even darker machine coming her way.

"It's a long way to San Gabriel," he said, roaring to a stop beside her. "The offer still holds."

Edwina didn't like anything about the vibrating death trap he rode, especially the earsplitting noise it made. But if she felt some trepidation, she felt even more relief. She still didn't know where on earth she was, and the balls of her feet were killing her. Uneasily, she took the hand he held out. He brought up his arm—the very same brawny arm that had pinned Mad Dog—and she found herself seated on the bike's passenger pillion behind him.

"Grab hold!" he yelled, revving the motorcycle's engine.

"Grab hold of what?"

"Me, Princess," he said sardonically. "It's like riding a horse. It works better when you hang onto something."

She grabbed for the side ties of his leather vest and felt them come loose as soon as the bike surged forward. Swaying backward from the powerful thrust of the machine, she nearly toppled off the bike. It was her stranglehold on his vest ties that saved her. She dragged herself forward and lunged for his torso like a drowning woman grabbing for a life raft. Throwing herself against his muscled back, she wrapped her arms around him and closed her eyes.

"That's right," he said, laughing.

He spiked the accelerator, and they shot off down the road.

I don't like this, she thought.

He responded as though he'd read her mind. "Relax. It sneaks up on you."

The curves were the worst part. Every survival instinct Edwina possessed told her to veer away from the arc of the bike, away from its squealing tilt and torque.

"Lean into the curves!" he shouted as they swooped down the narrow mountain road. "Let them take you."

"Let them *what?*" Jagged cliffs and scrubby pine trees flew by Edwina in a blur. "I can't lean!" she screamed back. "I'm paralyzed!"

"Hang on!" He negotiated a sharp S-curve expertly, slowing on the stretches, accelerating to take the curves. Edwina buried her head in the back of his vest and let out the wretched moan of a cornered animal.

Moments later she felt the bike slowing, coming to a stop, but she couldn't unlock her frozen limbs from their viselike hold on his body. "Are we there?" she whispered.

"We're never going to get there unless you loosen up a little," he said, traces of amusement in his voice. "You can let go of me now."

Edwina was stuck to him like a taffy wrapper, her heart still pounding in her throat, her hands clutching at his half-naked body. Frantic sensory signals from her brain told her that her fingers were not only digging at the granite muscles of his stomach but were tangled wantonly in his body hair.

I don't like this either, she thought. The task of peeling her moist body from his torso took all of her attention, but she managed three words. "You stopped. Why?"

"You need some coaching," he said, swinging off the bike and turning to help her.

She took his hand and landed on both feet with a bad case of rubber legs. It was all she could do not to drop to her knees and kiss the earth. Speed and fast curves had always terrified her. She'd never enjoyed carnival rides as a kid.

"You okay?" he asked, steadying her.

"Give me a minute . . ."

Diablo was surprised at the shimmer of fear in her eyes when she finally looked up at him. He released her hand, an odd smile burning in his throat as he quelled an impulse to touch her ashen face and reassure her. She was really frightened of the bike.

"Hey, take it easy," he said, laughing softly. "Nobody's going to get hurt." He would have to watch himself with this one, he realized. There was a trapfall of vulnerability hidden under her "purposeful" nature. A careless man could wander right into it and never find his way out.

Diablo allowed himself a moment to contemplate the pleasure of getting ensnared before he put the thought out of his head. He had a plan to put into action once he gained entry into the Warlords, a very dicey plan, and its success depended on the club members believing that he was one of them. Macho bikers did *not* wet-nurse frightened women.

However, he thought, contemplating her huge amber eyes, it was possible that *this* frightened woman might prove useful. He combed his hair back and glanced up at the blazing August sun before reconsidering her. "You could have dumped us both," he said brusquely.

"Sorry, I'm not used to switchback turns at warp speed." Edwina tried to inject a little sarcasm into the comment, but she was too shaken up to be anything but sincere under the circumstances. She was also confused. This biker person could be rude, he could be domineering beyond belief, but for a second there, she thought she'd detected a gentle quality in his voice. She must have been hallucinating. Terror could do that to a person.

"A motorcycle can smell fear," he said, patting the bike's tank as though it were a restless, snorting horse. "You've got to let it know who's boss, know what I mean?"

No, Edwina didn't know what he meant. She didn't have a clue about how to handle a several-hundred-pound motorcycle. Nor did she want a clue, and she told him so. None of that infallible logic seemed to impress him, however. Within just moments, he had her back on the bike and sitting in the driver's seat.

"I can't drive this thing!" she said as he got on behind her.

"Sure you can. Once you've got the feel of it, you'll be dangerous." His voice was soft and raspy in her ear, his arms an enveloping presence as he leaned forward to place her hands on the rubber grips. Even if Edwina could have driven the thing under normal circumstances, she couldn't possibly do it with him bending over her, breathing down her neck. She could feel him everywhere, down to the base of her spine. She could feel his powerful inner thighs hugging her hips!

"Give me a break!" she pleaded.

"The lady wants a break?"

Breathing laughter, he obliged her. He removed his hands and placed them on her waist. It was a simple movement that nearly took her breath away as she glanced down at the hands that spanned her midriff. Either she was awfully small or he was awfully large. His long tanned fingers all but met in the middle.

"Let's go," he said, directing Edwina's attention back to the task at hand.

She scanned the bike's bewildering equipment. "What do I do first?"

"Twist the ignition key, then disengage the clutch. When you've done that, open the throttle a quarter to give her some gas and shift into low gear. The last thing you do is open the clutch. Gently—very gently."

She craned around to look at him. "Huh?"

It wasn't like riding a bicycle, Edwina discovered. The throttle was on her right-hand grip, the clutch was her left, and her gearshift was the pedal beneath her left foot. Not exactly driver-friendly, she decided, struggling to master the essentials as he went over them with her several times.

"If I haven't got it yet," she said finally, "I never will."

"Let's give it a try."

She took a deep breath and twisted the ignition. The beast shivered, rumbling to life. Vibrations rippled through her like tiny tremors after an earthquake. It was frightening—the power. But tantalizing too. She depressed the clutch, gave it some throttle just as he'd told her, and once she had the bike in low gear, she opened the clutch.

"*Gently,*" he said.

The bike snorted, jerking forcibly. Startled, Edwina released the clutch altogether, and the huge machine burst forward like a launched rocket. Her fierce grip on the handlebars kept her astride, but her passenger wasn't so lucky. The surge nearly jolted him off the back end. Uttering a choice word, he caught her by the waist and righted himself, much as she had earlier. He dragged his boots along on the ground, steadying the beast as it shuddered and died.

She sneaked a glance at him. "It works better when you hang on," she said.

"Watch that sweet mouth, Princess."

Edwina soon realized it would take more than one session to teach a massive motorcycle who was boss, but once she had the machine powered up and going, it was more or less smooth sailing.

"I'm pretty good, aren't I?" she called out to him a short time later as they buzzed down the road.

"You're okay," he said.

She pulled the bike to a stop and cut the engine. Swinging around to smile into his dazzling green eyes, she was thrilled when he smiled back. "I'm damn good," she said.

His eyes went breathtakingly sexy then. Dark lashes lowered, accenting the electric green of his irises. Anticipation swept Edwina, leaving her light-headed in its wake. His mouth parted, and she thought he was going to kiss her. Instead, he slid off the bike and stood in front of her, hooking his thumbs into his jeans. "Now can we trade places and get where we're going?" he asked.

"Okay . . ."

"Trust me?"

His husky question nearly gave her a case of the shivering fits. Its meaning seemed to take on scope as he stared down at her. His sexy, shuttered expression could have implied anything, everything, so much more than a motorcycle ride. Trust him? What was she trusting him with when she got on the back of his bike? Her body? Life and limb? Somehow it felt as though the very things she held most precious were at stake.

He held out his hand.

After a lifetime's prudence—and a moment's indecision—she took it.

•　　•　　•

Once she'd gotten the hang of the curves, the remainder of the ride down the mountain was one of the most exhilarating experiences of Edwina's twenty-six-year-old life. She'd never been a risk taker in the reckless sense, but there was nothing else to call jumping on a Harley Davidson motorcycle with a stranger in black leather. It *was* a risk, and somehow that made every second of the ride more breathtaking. Adrenaline flowed in her veins.

She kept her head up and her eyes open this time. Her body absorbed the motorcycle's grinding velocity and its reverberating power, loving the speed, though the fear never left her. And finally, high on the adrenaline, she pulled the rubber band off her ponytail and let her hair fly free the way his did.

Only his naked stomach remained a troublesome issue. She couldn't get used to the way muscles rippled and flexed under her fingers when he moved. Even when he didn't move! She certainly didn't have the option of placing her hands higher, or lower.

"We're ten minutes away," he called back to her.

Ten minutes? Where had the time gone? Edwina felt a certain disappointment in knowing the ride was nearly over. But it was quickly replaced by a growing sense of purpose. She had a missing heir to find, and the man she was hanging onto might be able to help. *If* she could collect her wits and think of a way to pitch the idea to him.

When they rolled up to her hotel a few minutes later, she slid off the bike quickly before he could dismount.

"Thanks for the lift," she said, smiling as she fingered the chrome on the handlebars. She'd always been abominably bad at flirting, but her femaleness was the only bargaining chip she thought he might respond to.

"No problem," he said.

"And for showing me how to drive your bike."

"No problem."

She stopped fingering the handlebars and met his curious emerald gaze.

He leaned back casually, continuing to observe her as he propped his boot on the handlebars and flicked back his long black hair with a toss of his head.

Mr. Easy Rider, Edwina thought. Sexy. Cocky. A man with the kind of inborn arrogance that women loved. Probably had to beat them off with a stick.

"Will you come up to my room?" she asked.

"Your room?"

"Yes, I have a proposition to make you."

"What's your name?" she asked, stationing herself at a balcony window across the small hotel room from him.

"Is it relevant?" He shut the door behind him and leaned against the doorframe, looking indolent and intimidating all at once.

"The barmaid at Blackie's called you Diablo."

"I've been called that, I've been called worse."

"Diablo, then . . . I need your help."

He dismissed her with his eyes and began a slow, deliberate inspection of the room, opening closets and drawers, checking out her bathroom. When he got to her opened suitcase at the foot of the bed, he sorted through it dispassionately and then stopped with a look of disbelief.

"Now what the hell is this?" He lifted a two-foot rubber rattlesnake by its tail and dangled it in the air.

Edwina managed a quick dismissive shrug. "Doesn't everybody carry a rubber snake in their suitcase?"

He had just discovered her fallback plan. She'd learned through Chris Holt's high school yearbooks that Holt had two quirks in high school—a fear of snakes and an avid interest in astronomy. She'd packed the rubber toy, thinking she might use it to flush Holt out if all else failed.

"This could get interesting," he said, dropping the snake back into the suitcase. He resumed his sorting, and a moment later, with an intrigued glance at her, he hooked a pair of lacy white bikini panties on his index finger. Very skimpy panties. Not the sort of thing a woman with sensible shoes wore.

Edwina felt her stomach go tight. "Did you hear me?" she said. "I need your help!"

"I heard you." He turned to her, his green eyes oddly luminous. "Do you know what *diablo* means?"

"*Devil*, I guess. In Spanish."

He considered the panties dangling from his finger and then dropped them back in the bag. "And do you think the devil, Spanish or otherwise, makes a habit of helping uptight, *uptown* women?"

"He might," she replied sharply, "if the woman had something he wanted."

A faint smile flickered. "A bargain with the devil?"

"Help me find the man I'm looking for, and I'll make it worth your while. I have money." Edwina felt bubbles of hysteria building inside her. What money? She was so broke, they were about to repossess her house!

"What did he do to you, this Holt dude, run out on the wedding? Leave you pregnant?"

His eyes brushed her stomach, and Edwina wanted fervently to slap him. "It's nothing like that," she said, keeping her voice even. "This isn't personal. It's business."

She met his stare and held it defiantly, fighting the urge to look away. She was angry at his cavalier treatment, and yet she had the oddest sensation of being drawn toward him, sucked into his energy field, even though she hadn't moved or even breathed. "Will you help me? Yes or no?"

Edwina had no way of knowing that the man she was bargaining with had his own reasons for considering her proposition. Diablo turned and walked to the window, increasingly aware that Edwina Moody might be useful to him in a number of ways, including helping him gain entry into the Warlords. She didn't look like a biker's woman, but that could be remedied. What concerned him more was her inquisitiveness. He couldn't take the chance that she might discover his own reasons for wanting to join the gang. Beyond that she could get them both crucified if she continued to blunder around openly, searching for lost bikers.

He turned back to her, wondering if she was worth the trouble. Her eyes were still sparkling with anger, but that wasn't the emotion that was driving her, he realized. It was something else . . . anticipation. Even desperation. Her hands were knotted against her stomach, and her lips were parted expectantly.

Interesting, he thought. Maybe she needed him even more than he needed her. If that was the case, there were ways to keep her in line. He didn't particularly like the idea of frightening her, but he would if that was what it took.

"Maybe we can help each other," he said.

"How?"

"If this Holt you're looking for is a biker, he'll turn up at one of the bars, or at the bikers' rodeo in Holy Jim."

"Rodeo? When is it?"

He shook his head. "Not by yourself, Princess. You wouldn't last two minutes."

"I can handle it."

"Right. The way you handled Mad Dog."

"Okay, then . . . I'll go with *you*."

He smiled lazily. "Great minds."

Edwina could hardly believe her good fortune. "You'd take me with you?" She unlocked her hands and started toward him. "Really?"

"Sure. There's just one catch."

She slowed up, suspicious of the smile she saw brewing in his eyes. Wicked, that smile. "What?"

"I need a woman."

A slow headshake. "Ohhh, no."

A slow nod. " 'Fraid so."

Edwina gauged her chances of talking him out of whatever he had in mind and decided the odds weren't running in her favor.

"I like a good bargain as well as the next woman,"

she said, backing toward the French window behind her, "but not when the sale merchandise is me."

"You'll like this," he said, starting toward her.

She flipped the window's lock and flung the panels open. "Don't come any closer! If I scream, the whole damn town hears it."

The lazy smile reappeared. "A screamer? I like that in a woman."

"Help! *Fire!!*"

Diablo caught Edwina in one fluid stride, dragged her back inside, and clamped a hand over her mouth. "You want to get us thrown out of here?"

She wriggled free of the hand that muzzled her. "No—just you! You rapist!"

He jerked her to him, flush against his powerful body. "Nobody's going to rape anybody," he said. "You want stud service, go get yourself a brainless hulk like Mad Dog. That's not why I'm here."

Edwina fought to catch her breath. "Then why *are* you here?"

"I need an old lady." He released her and even took the time to straighten the collar of her blouse before she slapped his hand away.

"The Warlords have a run down to Rosarita Beach planned, and I want to ride with them. Their rules say no old lady, no ride."

"Old *lady?* You want me to be your *old* lady?" She shuddered delicately, almost unaware that her eyes had drifted from his face to the hair that curled in the opening of his vest. She caught herself following the dark diamond as it traveled down his body, a sensual directional signal for points south.

"What does an old lady do exactly?" she asked, coloring as she turned away.

"She rides with her old man, cooks for him, sleeps with him."

She turned back. "But you said—"

"I know what I said, In your case, we'll go for two out of three. You handle the riding and the cooking, and we'll fake the rest."

"Fa—" She couldn't get the word out. "Why don't

you just take me to the rodeo, and we can *forget* the rest?"

"You're missing my point, Princess. I want to ride with the Warlords, and you're my ticket in. You want Holt, and I'm the only safe way you're going to find him."

"But I can't go to Rosarita Beach—wherever that is! I don't have time! And what about the rodeo?"

"The rodeo's on the way. If you find Holt there, you're free to go."

Edwina was instantly suspicious. He must want to get into the Warlords very badly if he was willing to use her as a decoy. "What's so important about this Rosarita Beach run?"

"I've got my reasons, you've got yours." He exhaled, as though questioning the wisdom of their bargain. "Let's get a couple of things straight. You don't ask me questions, I don't touch your body, and we're both happy."

"I'd be free to pursue my investigation?"

"As long as the Warlords don't catch on. I wouldn't flash that picture again if I were you. And no obvious questions."

Edwina turned to the window with a nervous sigh. Here we go again, she thought, the proverbial rock and a hard place. She'd been faced with several wrenching decisions in the last year, and she'd always chosen in favor of her family's situation. However, this time her very life might be at stake. Certainly her virtue, such as it was.

"The Warlords hit the road tomorrow morning," he said. "How about an answer?"

For all her ambivalence, there was only one answer. She massaged her taut neck muscles and turned to him slowly, aware more than ever of his advantages over her in size and physical strength. What did the Warlords call a man like him? A rogue biker? It seemed inconceivable to her that she was about to entrust herself to such a man, perhaps in ways that she couldn't even imagine.

"Looks like you've got yourself an old lady," she said.

She wasn't sure what reaction she expected from him, but it wasn't the skeptical once-over he gave her. He took in her blouse, slacks, even her penny loafers, with a slightly pained expression.

"The outfit's got to go," he said.

She glanced down at herself. "What's wrong with my outfit?"

"Nothing, if you're a meter maid."

"Is that necessary?" Edwina jerked a wad of her own clothing from Diablo's hand, threw it back in the suitcase, and slammed the suitcase lid, nearly catching his fingers.

"If you want to ride with the Warlords, it is." He flipped the lid open again and resumed rifling through her things. "There's got to be something in here that's female and sexy."

He pulled out a white-cotton top and smiled. "This might work. And these." He tossed her the top and a pair of jeans. "Cut off the legs."

Edwina caught the clothing. "Hey! These are new jeans!"

"Yeah, that's a problem, but we'll make do." He looked her up and down, exhaled, and raked a hand through his long hair. "It's going to take some imagination, turning you into a hot number. Make those cutoffs short."

Moments later, Edwina emerged from the bathroom in jeans she'd altered jaggedly with her manicure scissors. The T-top was actually a ribbed cotton undershirt that was much too thin and snug for her liking. Diablo didn't seem to like it either.

"Lose the bra," he said.

Edwina's hands flew to her chest. "I can't do that!"

"The bra goes. Or you do."

"You're perverse!"

"Have it your way," he said, starting for the door.

"All *right*!"

Edwina hated him at that moment. However, when she emerged from the bathroom for the second time, it was sans bra. She blushed wildly at the way he looked her over, lingering on her unfettered breasts before he nodded approval. She felt naked, absolutely naked with her bosom straining against the skimpy stretch fabric and her legs hanging out of the cropped jeans.

Displaying herself so blatantly was akin to torture for a woman who didn't remove her towel until she was safely inside the shower stall with the door shut. And that was in her own bathroom! Now, in this strange hotel room, a continent away from her ruffled-chintz bedroom in Connecticut, she was exquisitely aware of her flesh heating under a stranger's scrutiny, her nipples tightening.

"Being ashamed of your own body," he said, fastening his emerald eyes on her as he hooked his thumbs in his pockets. "That's perverse."

"I'm not asha—" She sighed, knowing it was no use. There was a difference between taking pride in one's body and the exhibitionism he was demanding of her, but she had no idea how to explain that to him. Anyway, she probably was a little uncomfortable with her body. So what?

"Get your things together, and let's go," he said.

"Tonight?"

"Tonight. The Warlords should be setting up camp by now."

"Camp? We're going to be camping? Outdoors?"

His quick grin had a raffish quality to it that might have been charming under other circumstances. "It's no fun camping indoors," he said. "Come on."

Three

Some men loved the adrenaline rush that came from mastering the road on a powerful machine. Some men loved the horsepower. Diablo loved the freedom. The sensual purr of the motorcycle beneath him, the wind whipping his hair as he careened toward a bend in the road that led to parts unknown—he never got enough of it. Freedom was the drug that altered his consciousness and stirred his blood. Nothing else came close . . . unless you counted sex.

They were southbound along the coast, he and the woman, and the August sun was splashing down into the ocean like a space capsule on reentry. Blazing reds and oranges bathed the twilight horizon as he arced into an ascending curve that would take them into the hills. She let out a soft cry and held him tighter. At least she wasn't screaming. Things were improving.

It had been a long time since he'd had a woman behind him, nestled right up against his butt, her hands soft on his body. He'd forgotten how good it could feel. Warmth stirred deep in his groin, and his hungry thoughts quickly took the sensation to its logical physical conclusion. A hard man, a soft woman, and some tender sex. Tautening muscles reminded him how long it had been. And how righteously good it could be.

He hit the throttle and gassed it, spinning the bike onto a remote canyon road. Wind bit at his face, forcing him to rein in his bike and his fantasies. Just as well, he thought. Despite her valentine-heart mouth, the woman clinging to him like Saran Wrap was as uptight as they came, probably a virgin, for God's sake. Guilt twanged inside him, sharp and sweet as a country-western guitar chord. Maybe he should have told her what he had in mind for tonight?

Some fifteen minutes later they reached the area where Diablo planned to set up camp for the night. It was secluded enough that they wouldn't be disturbed and isolated enough to give her a taste of what the Rosarita Beach run with the Warlords would be like. She didn't know it yet, but she wasn't going to be meeting the biker gang until tomorrow.

He pulled the bike to a stop and dismounted, resisting the urge to help her as he set the kickstand. No self-respecting Warlord helped his woman off the bike. Any poor sucker who tried would probably get his hand bitten off for his trouble, Diablo thought wryly. A biker's woman was tough as carpet tacks.

"That was fun," Edwina said, surprising him as she swung her leg over the bike and smiled. She didn't look as though she needed help of any kind. In fact, with her windstung lips and hair blown blond and curly all over her head, she looked like a cross between Madonna and a fallen angel. Now that's sexy, he thought.

Almost involuntarily he made a quick inventory of her other assets—legs, breasts, and big brown eyes—and realized he'd created a mantrap. Sexy? She was *dangerous*, though he doubted she would believe him if he told her. Another awareness hit him as pried his eyes from the T-shirt that clung to her breasts. The Warlords would never recognize her as the woman who'd created a riot in Blackie's that afternoon. He wouldn't have recognized her himself. A smile crossed his lips. Maybe this was going to work out after all.

"So? Where are the Warlords?" she asked, squinting into the darkness beyond him.

"Later," he said dismissively. "You're going to need a little more work before I spring you on the gang."

" 'Work'?" It was a soft, surprised question that made her look even more adorable.

On impulse, he caught hold of her by the waist and lifted her away from the bike, aware of the delicate shiver of her breasts and the sleek line of her thighs. His palms slid up her midriff, and his thumbs nestled into the creamy drift of her breasts as he set her on the ground. Lord, but she was soft, he thought, letting his hands linger on her body as he stared into her copper-flecked eyes. Dappled with rust and gold, they were closer to russet than brown. Odd on a fair-skinned woman. Odd and beautiful.

"There are a couple of things you need to know," he said.

" 'Things'? What things?"

The smile never left her lips, but a strange sparkle of energy lit her expression. Fear, excitement? He couldn't tell, but her heart was beating out of control. He could feel it near his thumb. Blond tendrils of hair were caught in the dampness at her temple. It gave her a wild, flushed look that a man could take for panic . . . or for sexual desire.

"You're too soft, Princess," he said, his voice husking. "We've got to toughen you up some."

"Bikers don't like women soft?"

He would have laughed if she hadn't seemed so serious. Bikers' women were tanned and toughened from so much time riding under the open sky. Bikers' women were street-smart. This one was as fair and tender as a high school freshman.

"I like women soft." Lord, what an understatement. He nestled his thumbs into the silky curves of her breasts and felt his groin muscles tighten as though on cue. He'd give his right lung to have her sweet naked body all to himself, his to command for a couple of hours. The need to feel that kind of tenderness pressing up against him, pressing in *around* him, was almost painful.

"Well, that's a relief," she said, her voice breathy.

Her russet eyes were dreamy and a little drugged. They were whispering the very things that a hungry man wanted to hear—that she was susceptible and a little off-balance. That she was slightly drunk on rpm's and conquered fear. That she was feeling the blood rush hot in her veins, perhaps for the first time. That she liked it and wanted more.

One part of him didn't give a damn for anything but getting her flat on her back and making love to her warm, delectable body until dawn. Her parted lips and droopy lashes were telling him everything he needed to know. She had the same thing on her mind that he did. The problem was, he couldn't help wondering how long it had been since she'd been with a man. Maybe because until this very moment she hadn't looked like a woman who had *ever* slept with a man.

What's with this innocent? he wondered. Drugged or not, didn't she know she was supposed to run screaming from a guy who wore black leather and rode a monster motorcycle?

"I mean," she added, "if you didn't like soft, that would be a problem, wouldn't it? Since I'm clearly . . . soft."

Diablo felt muscles swell and harden at the base of his body. Blood surged through his heart. Clearly, *he* had a choice. And there was going to be a price to pay either way, he realized grimly. He could take her now, tonight. And to hell with their bargain. If she wasn't completely willing, he was damn sure she could readily be persuaded. However innocent, any woman who gazed at a man the way she was gazing could be persuaded.

Or . . . he could play it safe.

He couldn't believe he was even considering the latter, but in her case it just didn't feel right. She was homespun, sort of "nice." And he knew only too well what nice women did after you made love to them. They got weird. They had second thoughts. They got clingy or weepy, and he couldn't afford either. She was his ticket in, but she could also screw up his plans royally if she got emotional and unpredictable.

No mercy, he thought, referring as much to himself as to her. Steeling himself against the violent protest of his own body, he stared into the dreamy amber depths of her eyes, and broke the spell. "Where the hell did you get the name Edwina?" he asked, his voice still husky. "It's got to go."

Her eyes turned coppery, and she stiffened under his touch. "It's my grandmother's name," she said, obviously affronted. "Edwina Dickerson, on my mother's side. We called her Binky."

'Binky'? He was thinking of making hot, sweaty love to a woman who called her grandmother Binky?

She shoved his hands away and twisted out of the tight space between him and the bike. "I suppose you could call me Ed," she said abruptly, "or Ejay. That's what my sorority sisters in Delta Gamma Phi called me."

"I've got some bad news for you, Ed. The Warlords aren't into Greek. They've got two rules and two rules only: Don't mess with a man's bike, or his woman."

"Really? In that order?"

"That depends on the woman." He pointed to the crest on his bike and the words painted across the gas tank: PROPERTY OF DIABLO. "That's my mark. Whatever I put it on belongs to me: my bike, my clothes . . . my woman."

Her eyes widened. "You're not serious?"

He gave her that slow nod again. " 'Fraid so, Princess. Without my mark, you're fair game. You want to risk it, it's up to you. But I can tell you right now, I'm not going to feel like dragging Mad Dog off your body every time I turn around."

Edwina crossed her arms over her chest like a shield. "A mark of ownership? That's barbaric."

"I don't make the rules."

"What am I supposed to do, slap a *Post-It* note on my tank top that says Diablo's Woman?"

"Not exactly."

"Well, thank goodness. I've never heard of anything so primitive—or sexist."

"The mark goes on your person, Ed."

"What?"

"Most of the women have tattoos on their—"

"Don't tell me!" Edwina staggered backward, prepared to make the sign of the cross if he came near her. "Nobody's tattooing my person anywhere!"

"Sorry, that's the way it's got to be, Ed—"

"No! No tattoos! My mother is not a well woman, and that would kill her. I could never go home again."

He walked to the bike, unzipped a section of his gearbag, and pulled out a packet. "Relax. I'm going to use this."

"What is it?"

"A semipermanent tattoo. It washes off eventually, kind of like hair dye." He waved the packet temptingly. "It comes with a very attractive skull and crossbones."

Edwina didn't like the idea, not one little bit, but she couldn't see any way around it at the moment. She needed to get to that rodeo and track down Holt—and she certainly didn't want to be fighting off Mad Dog at every turn. "Oh, all right," she said finally, presenting her right arm to Diablo. "Hurry up. Get it over with."

He pulled a plastic bottle from the gear and approached her. "Nice bicep, Ed," he said, clearing his throat as though for emphasis, "but that's not where the mark goes."

"Where does it go?"

"Left breast or right buttock, take your pick. If you don't like those choices, the inner thigh, either leg." He grinned at her rapaciously. "Never say the Warlords aren't flexible."

"That's disgusting, Mr. Easy Rider, just *disgusting.*"

After much glaring and muttering, she finally consented to being "marked" on the curve between her collarbone and shoulder, well above the left breast. Slipping the strap of her tank top off her shoulder, she closed her eyes and gave herself to the procedure. If she had to have her person violated, at least she didn't have to see the damnable amusement in his green eyes as he did it.

He swabbed her skin first, much like a doctor preparing for surgery, and then he applied a solution that stung a little.

"Ouch," she said, her eyes flying open. "You didn't say this was going to hurt. What are you doing?"

"Making the skin receptive to the dye. If it takes, we won't have to do this again, *capice?*"

She closed her eyes and clenched her jaw. Mother would love this, she thought. Katherine Moody's devoted eldest daughter was being tattooed by a black-leather biker named Diablo who spoke Italian.

The remainder of the procedure was painless, physically speaking.

"That's not my shoulder!" she squealed once as his hands strayed too near her breast. He apologized quickly, to her surprise, and was remarkably circumspect otherwise.

Diablo wasn't a whole lot more thrilled with the ordeal than Edwina. The light was almost gone, and it was difficult to see. Beyond that, it was tricky to get the tattoo centered in the soft curve below her collarbone without touching something he wasn't supposed to touch. Unfortunately he was aware of her body movements in the same way that a cat is aware of every quiver of a cornered mouse. It was tantalizing watching her breasts shimmy when she moved. Even when she breathed. It was hell. Sheer hell.

"Hold still," he said as she opened her eyes again to see what he was doing. "This has to look real."

"This is incredibly silly, don't you think?" She released an impatient sigh. "Is the gang really that primitive?"

"Beyond your wildest dreams," he said softly, putting the finishing flourishes on his design. "Voilà."

French, too? A multilingual barbarian. Edwina craned her neck to see what the artist had wrought. "Good Lord," she murmured. Her shoulder looked as though it were going up in flames. The black death's-head was engulfed in a crimson blaze. It was beautiful, actually. And very macabre.

"I'm marked," she said quietly, feeling very marked indeed. She felt the pull of his eyes on her and looked up slowly to meet his gaze. The intensity in his green irises pooled like liquid lightning, diffuse and cool.

The electricity inside Edwina was anything but cool. It crackled like the filaments of a megawatt light bulb. "I guess this means I'm safe now?"

Safe as a baby, he thought. *From everyone but me.*

Edwina felt a compelling urge to touch him. It confounded her, her willingness to take risks with this man, to surrender her guard. Perhaps it was some resistance she sensed in him that made her so reckless. Whatever it was, she was terrifying herself. What if she did touch him? And what if he took her up on it? Her heart went a little crazy at the prospect.

He tossed back his hair with a quick, graceful jerk of his head. His eyes brushed over the mark on her shoulder, and then he met her gaze again, quickly, illicitly, his green eyes sinking into hers as a stone plumbs deep, still water.

Edwina's pulse began to labor. She felt paralyzed under his surveillance, as though somehow, in the laser precision of his glance, he was able to probe her most intimate thoughts. It was the briefest of connections, but it penetrated every defense she had. He had uncanny eyes. Eyes that took possession of whatever they touched. And right now they were touching her. It was almost as though he had the power to strip away her emotional safeguards with a look, to stir needs and desires that she was only subliminally aware of.

Absurd, she thought, turning away. *Impossible.* She was a full-grown woman and certainly the authority on her own needs and desires. And yet the encounter had frightened her. Her heart was thundering against the fist she'd pressed to her chest. Threatened, she thought, that was the word. In the split second that their eyes had met, he'd threatened her, almost at some bodily level, and it had scared her half to death. Her drawn-in breath shook as she waited for him to break the silence that surrounded them.

"Let's set up camp," he said finally. He returned the tattoo packet to his gearbag, and when he turned back to her, his expression was unreadable.

There was very little else said between them as they prepared to settle in for the night. He built a fire and got some water from a nearby stream. She did her best with a freeze-dried envelope of beef Stroganoff, but the sauce never truly dissolved beyond pea-size lumps.

They ate for a time in silence until he decided he should begin to prepare her. "The Warlords are rugged individualists, which shouldn't surprise you," he told her. "They like to live off the land when they're on a run. They buy only what they can't hunt or trap."

Edwina suppressed a physical shudder as Diablo continued. Her revulsion for trapping wild animals sprang from earliest childhood. Her father had taken her for a walk in the woods near their home one Christmas morning, and they'd come across a half-dead snowshoe rabbit that had nearly chewed off its foot trying to get free. It was one of the most heart-rending sights Edwina had ever seen.

Quelling another tremor, she debated whether to mention the incident, and then she remembered something from her research on Holt. It was one of the odd bits of information she'd picked up from his high school yearbook, something about his having been in the Animal Conservation Corps in his freshman year. If Holt was an animal lover, she reasoned, it was possible that he shared some of her feelings.

Diablo had moved on to the Warlords' emphasis on club loyalty and brotherhood when Edwina interrupted him. "You don't mean they actually kill wild animals?" she said. "Rabbits and defenseless creatures like that?"

"Only what they eat."

His tone suggested he thought it was an entirely reasonable proposition.

"But that's no excuse," she said earnestly. "There are plenty of animals in the grocery stores that are dead already. Cows, chickens. Couldn't they eat those?"

"It's not the same, Edwina."

"You too, then? You hunt down rabbits and squirrels?"

"Edwina—"

Not only was he using her full name, but his voice held a distinct warning. Drop the subject, it said. What he didn't know was that this was a subject she couldn't just drop. She wasn't an animal activist or anything, but she couldn't stand to see anyone or anything hurt. She felt the pain as keenly as if it were her own. Beyond that, there was the possibility of connecting with Chris Holt in some way.

"Let's call it a night," Diablo said, pointedly changing the subject. He went to get the two sleeping bags he'd lashed to the back of the motorcycle, and once he had them unrolled, he zipped them together.

"Where do you sleep?" she inquired cautiously.

"Same place you do." He held up the double bag. "Coming to bed?"

She curled her legs up against her chest. "You go ahead. I think I'll sit here for a while. The fire's nice."

"Suit yourself." He rose and stripped off his vest. When he unsnapped his jeans and began to pull them off too, Edwina swallowed a little sound of despair and looked heavenward. She wasn't getting in that sleeping bag with him, even if wolves tried to drag her off into the night.

He stretched out in the bag and yawned elaborately. Edwina tucked herself into a cocoon, wrapping her arms around her legs for warmth and to avoid the man she'd made an uneasy alliance with. She stared into the fire and tried to concentrate on what she'd come to California for—finding Holt.

It seemed only moments before Diablo's breathing turned steady and deep, and Edwina was immensely grateful. As the fire burned down and the chill increased, she thought longingly of the cardigan sweater she'd packed in his gearbag, but she was reluctant to move for fear of waking him. Undoubtedly the safest plan would be to curl up right where she was next to the fire and try to sleep.

Lulled by the chirping of crickets, she rested her head against her knees and drifted off.

Edwina's eyes flew open and she jerked awake, her nerves nearly jumping out of her skin. She'd heard a rustling sound, the kind that sent the hair on her neck skittering for cover. Having no idea how long she'd been asleep, she scanned the silent darkness and saw eyes everywhere. The fire was nearly dead, and Diablo was still sleeping like a bear in hibernation. She considered waking him. Instead, she scooted a little closer to his sleeping bag and huddled up again for warmth.

An hour later, she was still wide awake, freezing and jumping out of her skin on a regular basis. The nightsounds were torturously loud now—yelps and hoots and screeches. And, of course, that slithery rustling. She glared at Diablo in the sleeping bag, wondering how he could sleep so peacefully. Didn't he know they were surrounded by demon dogs and succubi?

She wasn't sure when it was that she heard him call out her name. Well, not her name exactly.

"Princess," he said, "come here."

Shivering with cold, she looked up and saw him opening the bag for her, making a place in the warmth next to him. "Princess." He hadn't called her that in a very long time, it seemed. She rather liked the sound of it. And she was freezing.

"I'm not taking my clothes off," she said.

"Get over here."

Male body heat, Edwina decided as she crawled into the warm bag—they ought to bottle it. She curled up carefully, facing away from him, but she couldn't stop herself from shuddering and sighing with relief. If she hadn't been so frozen, she might have worried when he draped an arm around her middle and pulled her up against him. As it was, she reveled in the heat and strength of him. Next to her icy skin and frozen limbs, he was toasty hot and rock solid.

She could feel the hair on his legs and the muscles of his thighs pressed up against her backside. And when she snuggled into him, she felt the protective cradle of his arm against the underside of her breasts. Shouldn't be doing this, she thought drowsily, but it was lovely. So lovely.

Edwina woke slowly with the fuzzy awareness that she wasn't alone. Someone was touching her. Intimately. Even more intimately than the body molded to the curves of her back, a hand was molded to the curve of her breast. All this she knew without even opening her eyes.

The hand moved, massaging gently, rhythmically, long male fingers moving against naked female flesh. The combination of heat and slow languid motion were unbelievably sensual. Edwina felt a thrill that ran the length of her body. Her eyes snapped open, and she glanced down, horrified to see the outline of Diablo's hand *under* her T-shirt, blissfully cupping her breast.

"What are you doing?" she said, her voice a hoarse squeak.

"Hmmmm?" His index finger leisurely traced the aureole of her nipple, sending another forbidden thrill through Edwina.

"Stop that!"

The finger stopped tracing. "Say what?"

"Your *hand*—"

He mumbled and shifted slightly, as though coming to wakefulness, and it was only then that Edwina realized she had an even larger problem. He was aroused! Fully aroused if the solid object pressing against the back of her thigh was any indication. She froze in the grip of his intimate embrace, afraid to move for fear of triggering some uncontrollable animal response in him.

Men suffered from an excess of hormones in the morning. She'd read that somewhere. If she could remain still for a few more hours, it might wear off. Lord, she wished she had a better track record with this sort of thing. Her only experience in college had been quick, furtive, and unsatisfying, done more to relieve the supposed stigma of virginity than to satisfy any deep desires. It was a mistake she still regretted, an unfortunate first experience with sex that had undoubtedly colored her perceptions ever since. Especially since she'd never done it since.

I don't like this, she thought, glancing down at the hand that had resumed its erotic inclinations. Damn him, anyway. If the other part of him started moving, she was going to scream her head off.

"Princess?" His voice was rusty and low, a man who had sex—and plenty of it—on his mind.

"I'm getting out of this bag," she declared.

The next thing she knew, she was being pulled around to face him. His eyes were half-lidded with sleep and fringed with dark lashes she'd never realized were so thick. "What's going on?" he said.

"You tell me, mister. I'm not the one in a state of engorged animal lust. Get a grip on yourself, for heaven's sake." As soon as she'd said the words, she realized their double meaning and blushed wildly.

Diablo swore softly, fighting a grin. "It might be best if you did get out."

"With pleasure." She jabbed him more than once with elbows and knees as she scrambled. Once she was out, Diablo pushed to a sitting position and wrapped the bag around him. He looked tousled and sexy, his long dark hair falling in casual disarray around his tanned shoulders.

Edwina hugged herself in the brisk morning air. "You touched me, you know."

"Sorry. It must have been a dream."

"Dream, my foot. You've had your eyes on my breasts since I met you."

"Your breasts?" He smiled lazily, letting his gaze drift to her crossed arms. "Is that where I touched you?"

Edwina was glad she was covered. Even if she had believed him, she wouldn't have accepted dreaming as an excuse. What if he dreamed he was making love to her? Was she going to wake up one of these fine mornings and find him doing that?

Diablo accepted Edwina's skepticism stoically. He *had* been dreaming, an incredible dream about cradling a blond slip of a woman in his arms and fondling her soft spots. The dream had been so real, the woman so warm and delicious, it had put some starch in his underwear, so to speak. Stiff enough to pound nails, he thought wryly, aware once more of his condition. Now he knew why. He hadn't been just dreaming it. He'd been doing it.

"I'm going to wash up," Edwina told him, heading for the stream. "Please calm yourself down by the time I get back."

Diablo watched her leave. "I'll do my damnedest," he called after her, "but it won't be the same without you."

Lots of natural talent, that one, he thought, watching her bounce as she walked. Probably more than she'd ever use. It was a shame to let a fine body like that go to waste, but he couldn't afford to get distracted, not while he was awake, anyway. He had a

plan to put into action when the time arose, and if
his hunch was correct, things were going to get very
interesting once the Warlords reached Rosarita Beach.
In the meantime he still had some groundwork to
do, leads to follow up on, people to check out.

He felt a twinge of guilt about the possibility of
endangering Edwina and just as quickly dismissed
it. She'd propositioned him, not the other way
around. If he hadn't taken her up on it, she would
probably have made the same deal to some other
biker, one who might not have other priorities. Anyway, he had no intention of letting her ride with
him into Mexico, even if she hadn't given up her
search for Holt by then. Just as soon as he was
initiated into the club, he was going to send the
princess packing. For her own safety.

He sobered, wishing his glands would accept that
he wasn't going to get physical with Edwina Moody.
He wasn't sure how long he could keep his priorities
in line if she kept snuggling up to him the way she
had last night.

He was getting their gear together, completely
calmed down, by the time she returned.

"I think we should go for a hike," she said, looking
fresh and perky as she gazed up into the sun-
drenched treetops where acorn woodpeckers were
drilling their holes and squirrels were cavorting. Bor-
dering the riverside behind her, wildflowers bloomed
in profusion, and Monarch butterflies flitted with
careless grace.

Diablo shook his head, thinking that she looked
as artless as the butterflies. "Can't do," he said.
"We've got a date with the Warlords."

The Wild Bunch in Repose, Edwina thought as
she peered through the trees at the motorcycle gang's
campsite. The gang had bedded down for the night
in a picturesque meadow, and Diablo had stopped
the bike on a hillside to give her a look at them
before approaching.

"They don't look so fierce," she said, watching a couple of men throw a Frisbee back and forth. The smell of bacon and coffee drifted up to her, and she spotted women cooking over open fires at various campsites. There was a noticeable absence of children and pets, but otherwise the Warlords could have been having a potluck social.

Diablo pointed out a tall lean man with long hair and a bushy, graying beard. "That's Squire, the leader. He's the one you've got to impress. He'll try to scare you, but don't let him." He glanced over his shoulder at her. "Ready?"

Edwina nodded, as ready as she would ever be.

They rolled through the camp slowly, Diablo revving his engine as individual members of the Warlords acknowledged him with a nod or a wave. Edwina was the object of some hot-eyed stares, but nobody seemed to recognize her from the day before. For that she was intensely thankful.

Diablo stopped the bike at Squire's campsite, swung off, and strode up to the leader. They clasped hands like arm wrestlers, hooking thumbs and playing at throwing each other off-balance. Men and their silliness, Edwina thought. The Y chromosome strikes again.

In the meantime a crowd was gathering around her and Diablo's motorcycle. Her impulse was to smile at the group, mostly women, but she thought better of it. Somehow "politeness" didn't seem like an image they'd respect. She scratched at her arm and considered spitting on the ground. She might have done it if her throat hadn't been so dry. Attitude, she thought, lay on the attitude. She settled for a look that she hoped was sullen and unapproachable.

A slender, tawny Mexican woman approached her anyway, cautiously at first. "Are you Diablo's woman?"

"I might be. Who's asking?"

The Mexican woman smiled, her dark eyes flashing with humor. "Nice to meet you," she said, extending her hand. "I'm Carmen. Squire's wife."

Edwina was puzzled for a moment. Was she supposed to shake her hand? Something as civilized as that? "I'm Edw—Ed," she said, taking the proffered hand cautiously. She half expected to be yanked off the bike and flung over the woman's shoulder.

Carmen's smile widened as she shook Edwina's hand firmly. Smiling back, Edwina decided that Carmen was perfectly charming.

"Ed—over here!"

Edwina looked around and saw Diablo signaling for her. At least he hadn't said 'Heel,' she thought, sliding off the bike. The crowd followed her as she joined Diablo.

"Squire—my old lady," Diablo said.

Edwina flashed a brilliant smile at Squire and sobered just as quickly when he didn't respond except to look her over like a prize heifer. "Nice work," he said to Diablo.

"She does speak," Edwina pointed out.

Diablo flashed her a warning look, but Edwina merely smiled at Squire and extended her hand. He stared at her a moment and then grimaced and gripped it for one quick bone-crunching moment. The crowd murmured in surprise.

"You want to ride with the Warlords?" Squire asked.

Edwina nodded, massaging her hand. She was inordinately pleased that he'd addressed her, but she didn't want to blow her tough image. "Sure. Why not?"

Edwina caught Diablo's approval, and almost simultaneously she spotted something that nauseated her—the charcoal remains of a small animal that had obviously been last evening's meal. An acrid taste filled her mouth as she struggled with her responses. The need to say something, to express her revulsion, very nearly overrode her common sense, but she knew an impassioned speech would do more harm than good under the circumstances. Especially if there was a way to sound out Squire and the rest of them without inciting a riot. Holt might even be in the crowd, she realized. It wasn't the timing she would have picked, but she didn't have the lux-

ury of waiting for the right time. There was a tax
lien on her desk back in Connecticut, and the clock
was ticking.

"I'm a little uneasy about the food situation," she
said.

"Plenty of food," Squire assured her. "We got our-
selves a couple of raccoons last night."

Racoons? Edwina nearly gagged on the breath she
was taking. "Actually, that's what I wanted to talk
about," she said quickly. "Diablo tells me you hunt,
and—"

"Ed," Diablo warned softly.

Edwina was aware of the risk she was taking, but
Squire's cocked eyebrow told her the gang leader
was curious. If she could state her case, *carefully,*
she might be able to sway him a little and learn
something at the same time. It was a long shot, but
she had to take it.

"I know you like to hunt," she said, an appeal
coloring her voice. "But with so many grocery stores
around, it seems kind of unnecessary, killing wild
animals, doesn't it?"

"Ed."

"You one of those environmentalists?" Squire
asked.

"No—no I'm not. I just don't like the idea of shooting something that can't shoot back." She tried to
stem the conviction she felt and couldn't, not completely. "It doesn't seem quite fair, does it?"

Squire's brows connected in the middle. The pained
look in his eyes as he glanced at Diablo said more
than words ever could: *Where did you find this
hairpin?*

Diablo shifted his weight, and that's when Edwina realized her plan had backfired. He was angry.
She was going to be shot when he got her alone.

"Maybe she's got a point, Squire," Diablo said.

Edwina jerked around in surprise, her heart rocketing as the two men stared at each other in silence.

"Maybe you don't want to ride with the Warlords,"
Squire said at last, his voice gruff as he addressed

Diablo. "Maybe you'd like to ride with a gang that chows down at MacDonald's?"

A rumble of laughter rolled through the onlookers, and Edwina felt a quick surge of something that might have been relief—or hope. Squire had a sense of humor. Maybe it was going to be okay. It was only as Diablo turned to her that she realized the deep trouble she was in. His eyes were ablaze again.

Four

Edwina knew one thing for certain. If she and Diablo hadn't been surrounded by Warlords, she would have been in desperate straits—one-on-one with the devil himself. She didn't need Diablo's protection at the moment. She needed protection *from* him. The spark of hellfire in his eyes brought her a stark reminder of whom she was dealing with. She'd seen him in action, and she had no doubt that he was quite capable of violence if pushed too far.

He turned to Squire, his voice grim. "I'd like a word."

The two men strode away, and Edwina smiled wanly. "It must have been something I said."

Carmen smiled sympathetically but offered no reassurance.

As the throng dispersed and returned to the task of breaking camp, Edwina was left to her own devices. The fine hairs on her neck were still prickling from the quick fury she'd glimpsed in Diablo's eyes, but as she watched the two men talking in Squire's campsite nearby, she realized something. They were going to be heavily involved for a while—and that would give her the perfect opportunity to do a little detective work.

Ordinarily Edwina was a prudent woman, one who considered alternatives, weighed options, and took risks only when the situation warranted it. 'Better safe than sorry' governed her decisions. Certainly in any other circumstance she wouldn't have dreamed of doing anything as foolish as provoking an already furious male. However, with both Diablo and Squire preoccupied, she couldn't resist.

The risk of getting caught made her doubly cautious as she picked her way through a field strewn with sagebrush and golden California poppies. Careful to give Diablo and Squire a wide berth, she kept to the outskirts of the grounds and pretended to be taking a walk as she surreptitiously checked out members for any resemblance to Christopher Holt.

A spindly, bearded specimen hunched under a huge sycamore tree caught Edwina's attention. He was scribbling furiously on a newspaper, and from her distance she couldn't tell how old he was or what he was doing, but his intensity intrigued her. And he certainly had Holt's lanky build.

She'd barely started toward the man when a snort of derision stopped her. Basking in the morning sun not ten feet away from her, Mad Dog was reclined against the sissy bar of his customized low rider. She'd been so intent on the seated man, she hadn't noticed the other biker lounging by the thicket of willows.

An insinuating smile twisted Mad Dog's mouth, and sunlight glinted off his mirrored sunglasses. As Edwina shielded her eyes, she saw sunlight flash off another object, a rectangular chrome gadget tucked into his boot. She thought it was a weapon at first, but she didn't see any barrels or sharp edges.

"Like what you see, Blondie?" he asked, adjusting his pants the way macho types invariably did when they were trying to be vulgar.

Mad Dog didn't have to try. Edwina returned his beady stare, tossed him a quick insolent headshake, and continued her walk. Her defiant gesture was deliberate. She couldn't afford to let a predator like him smell fear, but it would have been an even bigger mistake to let him engage her in suggestive

conversation. At least he hadn't recognized her. The
spark she'd seen in his eyes wasn't awareness; it
was lust. Obviously one woman was as good as another to Mad Dog.

The figure huddled under the sycamore was oblivious to Edwina as she approached. He was younger
than she'd first thought, perhaps in his early thir-
ties at most, and his only resemblance to the rest of
the gang was a straggly beard and a Warlord's leather
jacket with the name Killer imprinted on it.

"Bingo!" Thrusting the paper aside, he began furiously tapping out numbers on a solar calculator. He
hit the total button and whistled. "Smoked the Dow
Jones again!"

A *Wall Street Journal* lay crumpled next to him,
the stock section circled and highlighted. He was
playing the market, Edwina realized. Her thoughts
began to whir as she scrutinized him. Holt had just
inherited his uncle's stock-brokerage business, among
other things. He would have been an M.B.A. if he'd
finished school. Holt would know how to play the
stock market!

"Excuse me," she said as the man looked up. Brown
eyes, she thought, checking off another similarity.
Light brown, perhaps even hazel in the sunlight.
His unkempt beard was exactly the sort of thing
someone trying to hide his identity would grow. Even
his bone structure seemed uncannily close—and the
stab of vulnerability in his eyes. But she couldn't be
sure. She needed to get a look at the picture of Holt
in her jeans pocket.

"You play the market?" she asked, sensing the
man's wariness. Edwina was still learning the advantages of being a female investigator, one of which
was the ability to be nonthreatening to the subject
and to disarm his fears quickly by asking "friendly"
questions. When he didn't respond, she smiled and
crouched next to him. "I do too, a little. I was curious whether Bechtel was up or down today."

The man's eyes flicked up above her head, and
Edwina froze as a shadow fell over both of them.

"Your stock is down, Princess. Way down."

Edwina didn't rise immediately. She couldn't. An electric current had arced through her at the sound of Diablo's voice, and she had to fight to regain her equilibrium. Her fingers shook as she pressed them against the ground to steady herself. Odd, how he had such a disastrous effect on her—everything from raw fear to melting sexual urgency. *Who is it that throws the switch and puts me out of control?* she wondered. *Is it him or me?*

"Bechtel?" the man asked, as though it was now his job to reassure Edwina. He picked up the paper, but she stopped him with a grateful smile. No use dragging him into her "domestic" problems.

She took a fortifying breath, rose under her own steam, and turned to face her own personal devil. Surprisingly, his eyes conveyed no emotion other than the cold flicker of arrogance she'd come to expect.

"Let's talk," he said.

"What happened?"

He didn't answer her until they were well out of earshot of the stockbroker biker. "We're on probation," he said. "Squire's agreed to let us ride with the Warlords as far as the rodeo. Then, *if* he's feeling generous, he'll let me take their final test for membership."

"Test?"

"The Cliff Ride."

"It sounds dangerous."

His features darkened as swiftly as though a cloud had dropped in front of the sun. "One more word about defenseless animals, and you'll know more than you ever wanted to about dangerous, Princess."

Edwina hung on tight as Diablo kicked the bike into high gear and opened it up with a quick twist of the throttle. They swooped up Telegraph Hill and careened down the other side, seeming to fly like a hydrofoil, just above the black ribbon of asphalt. Below them the city of Long Beach slumbered in the late-summer heat, unaware of the herd of bikers about to stampede through its environs.

The Warlords had been on the road for over two hours, riding the freeways to the ocean and then zooming down Pacific Coast Highway like so many bats out of hell. The run to Rosarita Beach had officially started that morning, and the entire pack was on the prowl—freeway outlaws, taking their share of the road right out of the middle.

The wind whipped Edwina's blond hair, and even though she could feel the strain of the bike's acceleration on her neck muscles, she welcomed the physical stress. Outlaws, she thought. Was she one of them? She smiled at that, bemused. Edwina Moody, no stranger to danger.

She wasn't sure whether her blood was rushing from the thrill of the ride or from pure fear-induced adrenaline, but she was definitely on some kind of natural high. Even her fingertips seemed to be trembling in rhythm with the cycle's vibrant energy bursts. The machine gave off a finely tuned, barely perceptible vibration that moved through her limbs like light waves.

Moments later, as they pulled up to an intersection and stopped, she felt Diablo's stomach muscles contract under her fingers. She quickly relaxed her grip and managed a bright smile as he glanced over his shoulder at her. Maybe he wanted to call a truce? The smile died on her lips. No such luck. The banked anger in his expression carried enough electric potential for a summer lightning storm.

"I have this thing about helpless animals," she whispered, not wanting the other bikers to hear her. "I can't help it. When are you going to let me out of the doghouse?"

His eyes darkened. "Ask me nice."

Edwina never got a chance to ask him anything. The light turned green, and they roared off, Diablo cranking the throttle, and Edwina grabbing for his body. It bugged her that he always put her in a position of having to hang on to him for dear life. The fact that she *liked* hanging on to him for dear life was another problem entirely.

Her attraction to him baffled and amazed her. She couldn't explain its intensity unless it was a fascination with the forbidden. Rebels had never been her type, and yet everything about this one was rivetingly sexy, from his torn low-slung jeans to his mercurial green eyes. Foremost on her mind was his physical condition when they'd awakened this morning. She could still feel the heat of him pressed against her back, his hand caressing her breast. Remembering now gave her a hard jolt of longing.

A painful shock of excitement took her as he geared into low and they roared around a curve. Edwina felt vibrations penetrate clear through to her spine. No wonder she was so twitchy and overstimulated. It was the bike, she realized. His motorcycle was rolling foreplay.

By the time they reached their destination in the Santa Ana Mountains, she was limp as a kitten from physical sensation. It had been a grueling ride for someone new to the rigors of long-distance biking. Exhausted, she rested her canvas tennies on the upper footpegs and leaned against the bike's padded sissy bar as Diablo followed the pack to the campsite.

They rode through a beautiful heavily wooded area that bordered on a rushing river. Edwina took one look at the swirling blue water and wanted to wade in, clothes and all. It wasn't just her imagination that had overheated. The temperature had been climbing steadily all afternoon. To her fevered brow it felt as if the mercury had peaked out somewhere in the mid-nineties.

Diablo seemed to have read her mind. He broke off from the pack as they pulled into the camping area and headed for a secluded area upriver from the rest of the gang.

"How about a swim?" he said as he pulled the bike into a lush grove of willows.

Edwina wanted desperately to feel the cool water all over her sweltering body, but she didn't have a suit, and neither skinny-dipping nor a wet T-shirt plastered to her breasts seemed like a safe idea at the moment. Even if he could be trusted—which she doubted—*she* definitely couldn't be.

"Maybe later, when we've set up camp," she said, slipping off the bike. As she hit the ground, everything protested, from the arches of her feet to the muscles of her inner thighs. She ached as though she'd been riding a horse all day.

Flattening her palms on her hips, she managed a couple of creaky steps—and came nearly face-to-face with Squire. He had a rifle slung over his shoulder, and he was flanked by two other Warlords, men Edwina didn't recognize.

"I'm gonna need your old man for a while," he said, speaking directly to Edwina. "We've got some hunting to do."

His eyes flashed a challenge. Even if Edwina had any doubt about his intentions, she couldn't have missed the rigid authority in his posture, the steel in his voice. He was daring her to defy him. All three of them were. They were waiting, baiting her with bullying looks.

Her stomach clenched, and she turned away, defying the danger signals in Diablo's eyes. She was beginning to hate the predicament she found herself in a lot. Grown men with beards who picked on small animals, motorcycles that had aphrodisiac properties and a tropical heat wave—she slapped viciously at her arm—complete with mosquitoes.

Edwina met Diablo's glance and answered his warning with one of her own. His eyes hardened to emerald shards, piercingly beautiful and frightening. Her throat gripped, convulsing on its own movement, but she held her ground. Don't go, she implored silently.

He flicked his head, tossing black hair. With a quick careless gesture, he dug a red bandanna from his jeans pocket and tied it around his head. He can be cruel, she realized, witnessing the coldness in him. He can kill just as mercilessly as they do, and probably for no better reason than to show off his prowess with a weapon.

"Set up camp while I'm gone, Ed," he said brusquely. He strode to his cycle, pulled a sheathed knife from his gear, and strapped it on his leg. Edwina shuddered, from both anger and revulsion. How could he do such a thing?

It was close to nightfall when he returned. Edwina had spent most of the day at war with her own emotions and the rest of it in a fruitless quest for anything she could discover about Christopher Holt. It seemed that all the men had gone hunting, and because of her scene with Squire, the women weren't talking. Even Carmen had been unusually reticent when Edwina posed a few "friendly" questions about the Warlords, making Edwina wonder if Carmen had been ordered to give her the cold shoulder.

Now Edwina had a small fire going and some packaged soup simmering. She'd also found a corn-bread mix that needed only water. Her efforts were more from principle than hunger. The heat and emotional turmoil had robbed her of an appetite, but she wanted it known that she had no intention of eating whatever the Great White Hunter brought back.

He surprised her by striding into the campsite in an uncharacteristically upbeat mood and dropping a gunnysack at her feet. "It's a jungle out there," he said, a slow grin breaking as she glared at him.

Edwina glanced at the sack, grimacing as she imagined the contents. "I was hoping the wildlife would get *you*."

"Is that how you talk to the man who's just brought you dinner?" He crouched next to the sack and stared up at her, an odd glint of amusement in his eyes. "If you're not going to cook it, I will."

"Cook it? Dear Lord!"

Diablo reached for the sack, but Edwina beat him to it. Spurred by sincere outrage, she whipped it from under his nose. "Nobody's going to cook anything," she said, her voice cracking with emotion. "I'm giving the poor thing a decent burial."

"You might want to take a look at it first."

A strange odor filled Edwina's nostrils, pungent and unpleasantly metallic. "What's in there?" She opened the sack and pulled out a good-size brook trout by its tail. "You let me think this was a raccoon?" she said, incredulous. "How could you do that?"

A devilish grin broke on his face, and Edwina couldn't help herself. He *was* cruel—cruel to make her believe he'd killed an animal, and crueler still to make fun of her distress. She took a backhand swing at him, fish and all. He ducked gracefully, dodging again as she tried a forehand. They both knew it was futile. He was much too fast for her, and that knowledge, with his hoots of laughter, drove Edwina crazy with frustration. She wanted to get the bastard so badly, she could taste it!

Occasionally the Fates take pity. Whatever the reason on this occasion, they smiled down on Edwina's plight with a certain poetic elegance. The very gunnysack that Diablo had brought the fish in became the instrument of his downfall. Literally. As Edwina menaced him again, his boot-heel caught in the slippery burlap. His feet flew out from under him, and despite an impressive effort to save himself, he sprawled on the ground.

Hard-packed clay. A large man. It was a nasty collision.

Edwina's surprise surfaced in a hiccup of laughter. Of all the fatal diseases and black curses she'd wished on him that morning, she'd never thought of having him slip on a bag and land on his fanny. She walked over and gazed down at him, knowing she should ask him if he was hurt. Unfortunately a different impulse came over her.

"How does it feel, Great White Hunter?" she said, placing a foot on his chest and dangling the sacrificial fish over his nose. She was pressing her luck, and she knew it. Whatever state of grace she might have enjoyed up to that point was rapidly ending. Even the Fates would have blanched at the wicked glint in Diablo's eyes.

"How does it feel?" he said. "You tell *me*."

He yanked her foot ferociously, and hop though she might, Edwina couldn't keep her balance. The fish landed in the river behind her, and she landed on Diablo.

Without divine intervention, she didn't stand a chance against him. He flipped her on her side, facing away from him, and pinned her arms behind her back before she could even think about struggling. "You need some lessons on being a Warlord's woman," he said, his breath hot near her ear.

Locking her up against his body with an arm around her midriff, he elaborated. "Lesson number one: Don't ever laugh at your man, Princess."

"You deserved it. You let me think that disgusting thing was a raccoon . . ."

His laughter was ironic. "What's this?" he said. "Edwina Moody, protector of all living things, doesn't love a fish?"

"It's not the same," she said. "Fish are . . . fish."

He brought her around to face him, green eyes sparkling as he recaptured her hands behind her back. "Could the trout help it he didn't have big brown eyes like a raccoon?"

"Now you're championing fish? You, who just killed one?"

They stared at each other for a long moment, both smelling pungently of fish oils and musky heat, and then they began to laugh. Softly at first, and reluctantly on Edwina's part.

"Lesson number two, Princess," he said, his voice shimmering with ardent undertones. "The clothes come off."

"What do you mean?"

He gripped her wrists tighter when she tried to pull free. "A swim in the river. We both smell pretty ripe."

Edwina could feel every inch of his "ripe" body

against hers, and the smell of fish was the last thing that concerned her. She knew unquestionably that if she took off her clothes and went into the river with him, it would escalate into the most abandoned interlude she'd ever had.

She knew it because she'd felt it beginning from the first time he'd trapped her in his hot green gaze. She'd felt it all, the rising tide of awareness between them, the swift and paralyzing intimacy, the building toward something inevitable. She couldn't even ride behind him on the bike without fantasizing what it would be like to make love with him. How would she ever survive the river—naked?

"I'll make do with a sponge bath." She remembered her shoulder and spot-checked it. "I don't want to mess up the tattoo."

"That tattoo," he said, his voice grating softly, "is *my* mark." Rolling her onto her back, he pinned her arms above her head and raked swiftly over her body with his eyes. Edwina nearly had heart failure as she imagined his intentions. The ground was rock hard against her shoulder blades, and she could feel the weight of the leg he'd dropped over hers, trapping her.

He studied her for another long moment before he released her. His eyes continued their indolent scrutiny, brushing over her with an intimacy that felt as physical as a stolen kiss. He scanned her breasts, lingering as her breathing quickened. And then he caught her lips in his gaze.

If Edwina had been standing, she would have buckled at the knees. There was a quality of rough seduction in his gaze that left her utterly weak. Lethargy crept into her muscles, saturating her with its soft ache. And yet she was trembling by the time he released her. Trembling with sensations so vibrant, they hurt her with their brightness.

He smiled faintly.

If ever a man knew he could have a woman, this one did, Edwina realized. And yet he didn't act on it. He combed his dark hair back negligently and rose to his feet, standing over her. With a quick motion of his hand, he brought her to her feet, his eyes flashing over her body with one last scorching look before he broke away. Edwina swayed unsteadily as he left her, as though the forces holding her up were being drawn off in his wake.

She could do little but watch him as he walked away—long, long legs and lean hips melting into the darkness. Once he'd disappeared, she sagged onto a log near the fire.

Gracious was all she could think. *Good gracious.* It was her mother's phrase, so ridiculously old-fashioned and yet oddly appropriate to the moment. Her heart was hammering, flooding her body with blood and heat and relief. She should have been grateful. *She should have been down on her knees, thanking the heavens for her deliverance.*

And yet . . . she didn't feel grateful exactly, did she?

She stared at the fire, and as her heart quieted, her mind quickened. What was happening to her? Why was she responding to him so unrestrainedly? He was threatening to her in so many ways, but she seemed to be attracted to the danger he represented, perhaps even to seek it out.

He wasn't the man she'd always dreamed about. He was the man she'd never *allowed* herself to dream about. The man she must have known instinctively would be her undoing. And yet how to explain these sweet, crazy stirrings inside her? Did she want to be undone?

She certainly didn't want to be one of those repressed women who melted helplessly under a man's touch, but that seemed to be exactly what was happening to her. Even now, in the aftershock of her immediate relief, she felt a warm listlessness stealing over her. She drew in a breath and held it, closing her eyes. Crazy, crazy woman—she wanted to be with him!

The admission flooded her with sweet stimulation. She rose to stare restlessly at the river, and within seconds, she was as softened and achy inside as a dreamstruck kid. It was true. She wanted to be with him. *And she wanted it badly.*

Conflict rose inside her as she gazed at the river. She hadn't come to this place for a reckless fling with a biker. She had a mission to accomplish, a man to find, a family to salvage. *Obligations*. Edwina Moody had obligations.

Remembering brought the full weight of her responsibilities down on her. She could feel them settling on her like a heavy coat, and at the same time, a kind of pain welled up in her. The truth—the naked, frightening truth—was that she wanted desperately to shed that suffocating coat, even if only for a moment. She wanted to ride on the back of Diablo's bike, her hair flying in the wind. She wanted to swim naked with him in mountain rivers.

Impulsively she went to the river's edge and slipped off her shoes, wading in up to her ankles. The water was so deliciously cool, beads of perspiration broke out along her brow and upper lip. She searched the river's silvery swirls and ripples for any sign of him, afraid she might find him, *afraid she might not*. The memory of his touch filled her with a sweet, aching longing, and at the same time, she dreamed of the water's coolness against her burning skin.

She began to wade upstream, more aware with every step that she was spurred by something deeper than conscious control. She needed to find him, that was all, and if she let herself dwell on what would happen when she did, she would lose her courage. She continued upstream as the water swelled and swirled around her, and within moments, the river's currents had strengthened dramatically against her movements. She rounded a bend, and the river sent up a roar. Opening onto a turbulent section of white water, it foamed and flashed in the moonlight.

It was a breathtaking sight. Under other circumstances Edwina might have stood there, entranced, for hours, but the currents pulling and tugging inside her were even more compelling. Unable to wade any further, she returned to the shore where she rounded an outcropping of rocks, climbed a grassy rise, and found herself staring at one of the most beautiful feeder pools she'd ever seen. Even in the moonlight the water's jeweled tones were evident—cerulean blues and Egyptian greens.

The water looked so irresistibly cool and inviting to Edwina's overheated sensibilities that she longed to plunge in. She even touched the zipper of her jeans, but her fingers froze as the water began to ripple and swirl across the pond. A small whirlpool of suction drew her attention, and then a form broke the surface, spewing geysers of water into the gleaming night.

The scene seemed to hesitate before Edwina's eyes. The moonlight crystallized to silver strands, and water droplets hung in the air like icy gems. The form flew upward, roaring and shaking, a rocket from Atlantis, a sea creature in imminent flight. Even before the water had cleared, Edwina knew it was he.

He shook off the excess water and threw his head back, flinging wet hair off his face. It cascaded down his back like heavy black satin, streaming water, deflecting light. Residual water defined the contours of his body, drenching muscles and body hair. Standing in the pool, sunk in reflected moonlight up to his hips, he was an awesome sight.

Edwina ducked back into the cover of the rocks and pressed a hand to the frantic noise in her chest. She had found what she was looking for. The question ringing in her head was what did she do *now*? She felt weak, almost faint, at the thought of approaching him. He was too wet, too naked, too male. She was losing her nerve. She hated herself for it, but whatever part of her had fantasized this moment was totally overwhelmed by the reality of it.

She waited until he sank back into the pool and began to swim lazily, rolling and submerging like a sea animal at play. The strongest impulse inside her was to leave, to run like crazy. *Now—while she still could*. If she disappeared around the rocks while he was under water, he would never know she'd been there. Her heart soared as she hesitated. She imagined herself slipping away soundlessly, vanishing into the darkness, running. And yet she didn't move.

He surfaced again, to a soft gasp of sound. His? Or her own? She couldn't run now. She was caught. He hadn't seen her yet, but he soon would unless she could become an inanimate as the rocks, unless she could slow her crazy heart and still her breathing.

She'd never done anything like this before—watch a man swim naked in the moonlight. A man who didn't know he was being watched. She'd never even seen a man undress, for that matter. What little furtive groping she'd done in high school and her one fling in college had all been accomplished in murky parked cars. Nothing like this. Nothing so stark and real. Nothing so beautiful.

The crazy excitement inside her made it almost impossible to continue looking at him, painful somehow. And yet she couldn't drag her eyes away. As he shook his hair and rose to his full height, Edwina realized he was coming ashore. Her stomach wrenched, and she averted her eyes as he waded out of the pool.

He wasn't twenty feet from her, water still streaming down his body as she looked up. It was unavoidably evident that he was built well, everywhere: long-limbed, superbly muscled, and ridiculously well endowed. He picked up his jeans and stood a moment, as though letting his body dry in the night air before he put the jeans on.

Edwina was helplessly fascinated by his apparent comfort with his nakedness. She found her eyes returning again and again to the spear of dark hair that knifed toward his groin—and lower, to dark male parts that gave her a thrill of fear.

Her heart began to pound almost violently, and finally it was too much for her. She couldn't look at him any more than she could force the image of him from her mind—his body glistening in the moonlight, sensual and pagan.

When she turned back, he was gone.

She scanned the area nervously, thinking that the flickering light must be playing tricks. When it became evident that he was really gone, she came out of the shadows. She didn't know whether to be relieved or disappointed.

She walked to the pool, staring at the lustrous sheet of light, and wondered if she would ever feel free enough to strip off her clothes and plunge into the water, or into life, with such abandon. She'd never been inclined toward self-indulgent pleasures in any form. They'd always seemed selfish somehow, even decadent. And yet Diablo seemed content to go where the wind blew him—no strings, no responsibilities, answering to no one. Was that self-indulgence? Or self-fulfillment?

Kneeling at the pond's edge, she filled her cupped hands and splashed cool water over her face and arms. She ached to feel that coolness trickle over her sticky breasts and midriff, but even if she'd had the courage, there wasn't time. He was undoubtedly heading back to their campsite, and he would wonder where she'd gone.

The moon seemed to flash with a peculiar brightness as Edwina rose to her feet. She hesitated, staring at the reflections in the pool, her own and—

Spinning around, she smothered a gasp as she saw him. He was standing near the outcropping of rocks where she had stood. And he was watching her just as she'd watched him.

"You knew I was there all along," she said, hardly able to speak.

"Turnabout's fair play, Princess," he said softly. "You had your stripshow. Now I want mine."

Five

A stripshow? Edwina stepped back, her bare heels sinking into the gently lapping water. "That's not funny."

"Who's laughing?"

"But we have a deal," she said, thinking quickly. "Hands off? No questions? It was *your* idea, remember?"

Diablo slipped his thumbs into the belt loops of his damp jeans, the only clothing he wore. The effect was to drag the unsnapped jeans lower on his hips, revealing a line of white skin that hadn't seen the sun. Edwina hadn't noticed it before, and in some strange way the sight was even more provocative than his nude body had been. Especially now that she knew what was inside those jeans.

He began to advance, and Edwina had the choice of backing more deeply into the water, standing her ground, or trying to outrun him. None of these seemed advisable, given the predatory glint in his eyes.

"Hands off, remember?" Her voice cracked, desperate. "If you break the agreement, then so can I."

"Who said anything about handling you? All I want is a show. I think I've got that coming, don't you?"

Edwina's pulse was frantic. This wasn't part of her fantasy at all, and yet something was riveting her in place, just as before. She couldn't have outrun him if she'd wanted to, but that wasn't what was holding her. It was the reason she'd come in the first place. It was what he represented—a chance to feel something that was free and uninhibited. Freedom was a frightening thing, she realized. *And irresistible.*

"Let's get the show on the road, Princess. Strip."

His rough command jolted her into action. She touched the strap of her T-shirt and averted her eyes, unable to look at him as she realized that she was going to do it. *She was going to take off her clothes.* She began to draw the strap off her shoulder, and the warmth of her sensitive skin brought her an unexpected shock of awareness.

She gasped softly as the hot sensation ran down the length of her arm, electrifying everything in its path—skin, sensory nerves, delicate bones and tissue. In its aftermath she felt raw and burned to the touch, as though she'd been exposed to the sun too long.

Dear God, she thought, *I don't think I like this.*

But her body didn't seem to care whether she liked it or not. Her skin was responding to the flood of nervous agitation with a tingling urgency. Warm and vibrant, her breasts seemed to be growing heavier by the second, lush with hormonal stimulation, her nipples rapidly contracting.

Edwina's next breath came too quickly, and her fingers froze on the strap. As much as she might want to go through with it, the prospect of exposing her *aroused* body to his eyes was almost painful to a woman as modest as she.

"We haven't got all night here, Princess."

He *could* be cruel, she thought. Couldn't he see how difficult this was for her?

She drew the strap off her shoulder and anticipated another electric shock, expecting the jolt of current like a child who'd just touched an open socket. She held her breath as it hit, a beautiful, wiry kind of pain that was almost unbearable. Her lungs spasmed, seeking air.

She shook her head, not looking at him.

"What's wrong?" His voice was taut.

"I *can't.*" There was a plea in her shaking declaration. Dizziness swept her as she tried to look up. Her mouth went dry, and her breath flooded in and out so fast, she couldn't tell if she was inhaling or exhaling. It might have been too much nervous stimulation or too little food. She hadn't eaten since breakfast, and yet it didn't feel like faintness.

Watching her from his vantage point, Diablo tossed back his damp hair. What the hell was she up to? She looked as if she were about to faint, and yet moments before, watching him from the rocks, she'd been devouring him with her eyes. He figured she had finally decided to come out and play, but maybe he'd been wrong.

Some women were difficult to read. This one was deadly. Her big brown eyes were full of erotic messages: *Take me,* they said. *Make wild love to me, drown me in passion.* And then whenever he got near her, she went limp as a baby. She was waiting for someone to sweep her up and take her to heaven. He'd known that from his first good long look into her enormous eyes, but he'd made up his mind *not* to be that man. The hell of it was that she'd been making him regret his decision ever since.

She brought a hand to her forehead, and he thought he saw her falter. "Edwina?" He reached her in seconds, hooked an arm beneath her legs and scooped her up. "It's all right," he said, wading into the pool with her. "I've got you."

He intended to revive her. Instead the chill water hit Edwina's overheated skin with a rush of cold that nearly threw her into shock. She clung to Diablo dizzily as the mountain became a carnival ride and everything began to swirl and blur around her.

"You okay, Princess?"

Edwina had no idea how much time had passed when at last the world stopped spinning and his voice wafted down to her again. "You okay?" he repeated, sounding husky and concerned.

She shook her head. "I don't . . . like . . . this."

He didn't quite smile, and the slight compression of his lips was infinitely sexier than if he had. "Let's see if we can fix that." Cradling her gently in his arms, he knelt and settled her weight on his bent knee, immersing them both to their shoulders in the pool.

Using his arm as a backrest, he began to work gently and steadily on the taut cords in her neck. Water pooled and eddied with his slow, rhythmic movements, and the combination of warm fingers and cool liquid flowing against Edwina's skin seduced her muscles into a state of thick, dreamy languor.

"Let me know when you like it," he said.

She gave a little gasp as he began working his thumb into taut shoulder muscles. "What happens when I do . . . like it?" she asked.

"Anything you want."

"You'll put me down?"

"If that's what you want."

A warning went off in Edwina's head. He had the tone of a man who was much too sure of himself and his sexual power over her.

"In that case, I do like it," she said. "Now, if you'll put me down . . ."

He moved a little deeper into the pool, releasing her in water that came up to her breasts. Edwina clutched at his arms, unsteady on her feet as she touched bottom. The pool floor was studded with small rocks, and she still felt a little woozy.

He caught her elbows, anchoring her. "Are you okay?"

She nodded, aware of the husky texture of his voice and, more gradually, of her fingers gripping the muscles of his upper arms. As the water lapped at her breasts and ribboned between her legs, she realized she was staring at the damp, downy whorls of hair that patterned his chest. A beautiful pattern, she thought, like wings. Her fingers tightened on his arms.

A peculiar thing was happening to Edwina as she stood in the water opposite him. Her body was cooling on the outside and warming on the inside. There was a flowing of sensation in the vicinity of her female parts that was uncannily similar to the cool stream of water around her, but it was several degrees warmer and somehow tender. It made her think of a bruise just beginning to swell, exquisitely sensitive to the touch.

Was it starting all over again? she wondered. The soft aching, the dreamy urgency that had brought her here? In a few more seconds, would she want him so badly she'd be lost?

"What if I wanted to leave?" she said. "Right now."

"Are you asking if I'd stop you?"

"Yes."

"Then the answer is no, I wouldn't."

Edwina searched his features. Would he really let her go that easily? Without a struggle? She saw the low-glowing wattage in his eyes, the muted charge of sexual energy, and suddenly she understood. He was willing to let her go because he knew she wouldn't go. He understood her weaknesses better than she did. Oh, she hated him for that. She hated him for knowing she didn't have the strength to walk away from him. *She hated him for knowing how urgently she wanted to be with him.*

She glanced down, shaking her head in self-reproach.

"I wouldn't stop you, Princess," he said. "But I might try to persuade you not to leave."

She felt him take her by the shoulders, and a sigh welled up in her throat. In her determination not to look at him, she was startled by the sight of her own soaked T-shirt clinging to her breasts. Wet cotton was stretched thin as tissue over her creamy flesh. Her nipples budded before her eyes, tingling almost painfully. She might as well have been naked, except that this was worse somehow, sexy glimpses of half-drenched skin that fed the imagination. Her head snapped up, and she caught him looking at her there too.

His dark lashes fanned upward as he raised his eyes slowly to hers. "Ever heard the phrase 'beautiful when wet'?" he said.

"I think that's '*slippery* when wet.' "

"Even better."

As Edwina registered the sexual meaning of what she'd said, the warmth inside her became heat. Taut, scarlet heat that stained her face as well. She ducked her head, reluctant to cooperate as he brought her face back up to his.

"Do something you're afraid of, Princess." He cupped her chin and stared into her eyes. "Just once. You'll live the thrill a thousand times in your mind."

She felt the thrill he spoke of deep inside, felt it lance through her like a spear. How did he know that was what she wanted? A tiny moan hovered in her throat as he stroked the trembling softness beneath her chin and bent to kiss her. His fingers were warm and demanding, his breath hot and sweet as he fitted his mouth to hers.

He stroked the underside of her chin, showering her with butterfly touches until Edwina yielded helplessly. She parted her lips, whimpering as he dipped his tongue into her mouth. He seduced her with light sidelong touches, probing slowly, almost languidly. Edwina went limp in his arms as he deepened the strokes. A frisson of excitement flared down her spine, melting her all the way to her toes.

"Just once, Princess," he murmured. "Just this once."

He caught her by the waist, nearly spanning the width of her with his hands. Cool water cushioned the heat of their bodies as Edwina let herself sway into him, hips first, sighing as her breasts crushed softly against his chest. She closed her eyes, reveling in the textures of him—sex-hardened muscle and silky wings of hair.

"I think I like this," she said.

"*Finally.*" A groan of satisfaction roughened his

voice, and he began to ease her legs open with his knee. "And this?"

Edwina felt a sharp thrill of alarm. Her thigh muscles resisted automatically. And then his husky voice seduced her into sweet submission.

"Come with me, Princess," he said. "We're going for a little ride, that's all."

She sighed a shocked, blissful sound and went weak with anticipation as he insinuated his leg between hers and brought his thigh up against that tender, vibrant part of her body. His gentle movements as he encouraged her to sit astride him sent dazzling currents of pleasure through her. It was as though he had thrown the switch that controlled all her responses, and she was instantly awash in sensations that she was helpless to stop. He had found the most vulnerable part of her body, and with the slightest pressure, he could send brilliant little starbursts rocketing through her.

"Easy, Princess," he said, gentling her with his hands as she reached for him. "Relax and enjoy the ride."

She softened against him helplessly, dizzy with pleasure as he began to rock her slowly and rhythmically. The heat of his muscles, the faint swaying motion, sent melting rivulets of desire through her. The sensations were so riotously sweet that she could hardly believe them. She'd never felt such deep, radiating pleasure. It was almost more stimulation than she could stand.

"No more." She breathed the words aloud. She could hardly believe what was happening. It was almost as though the feelings were taking control of her, as though *he* were taking control, sapping her strength with every slow spur of pleasure he gave her. It was good, *too* good, and in another moment she would be utterly defenseless against him.

"*No more,*" she pleaded.

Diablo heard her, but he couldn't stop. She was so exquisitely responsive. Every touch, every rocking movement, forced a sweet little cry out of her. Watching her come alive in his arms was the most irresistible thing he'd ever witnessed. She was no innocent, he told himself as she began to move and rock against him. He'd never known an inexperienced woman who responded as she did.

"Easy," he said, steadying her as she clutched at him. "Relax and let it take you, Princess. Just like the curves, remember?"

Edwina felt such a rush of hunger at the sweet jolts of stimulation that she gripped his arms fiercely and let out a panicky, anguished sound. The longing inside her was so sharp that she couldn't stop to think about why she felt it, or what she might logically do about it. There was only one thing to do at the moment—assuage the terrible longing, get as close to him as she could.

He slipped a hand inside her tank top and cupped her breast, compressing the tender flesh in his palms. His cool touch shocked her. He was both rough and gentle, and with each flex of his long fingers she felt as though something were being released into her bloodstream, a powerful drug.

Desire flared up in her swiftly, uncontrollably. It was like a torch touched to kerosene. An anguished moan slipped from her throat, and as he began to rock her faster, she pressed herself against him wantonly.

"Make love to me," she pleaded. "Please—*please!*"

"Easy, Princess."

Edwina felt his resistance and didn't care. She was in a fever heat. She had to touch him, feel him everywhere—on her, *inside* her. She was crazy with need.

Diablo felt her fingernails bite into his arms and knew something was wrong. Her cries, sweet before, sounded almost frantic.

"Easy, baby," he said, catching hold of her arms and holding her back. Almost as quickly as his brain registered the anguish in her face, his intuition told him what had happened. He had misunderstood her quick hot passion. Her urgency had fooled him into thinking she was experienced when she was actually deprived. This was her first time in a very long time, he realized. And he had already aroused her to the point of pain.

He lifted her up bodily and pulled her into his arms with an angry explosion of passion. "Damn," he said as she cried out, a sound that was heart-breakingly sharp. "Damn, how could I not have known?"

Edwina's eyes flooded with stinging tears as she shuddered in his arms. Deep muscles clutched inside her, and her body throbbed with tension. She was too badly shaken up to ask him why he'd stopped. All she knew at the moment was that he was a wall of solid warmth, and she desperately needed something hard to press herself against, something hard to relieve the awful clutching pain of desire.

He held her tightly, rocking her until finally the throbbing began to recede and a sigh of relief shuddered through her. Hearing it, he breathed an expletive and buried his face in her hair. His touch became momentarily rougher as he palmed her buttocks and pulled her even closer.

Edwina softened against him with a gasp of awareness, melting into corded thighs, jutting hipbones, and aroused maleness. Warm breath jerked in her throat as she realized what it must have cost him to stop as he had. He was aroused! He was every bit as hard as the rocks they stood on. Every bit as hard. Every bit as wet.

She looked up, silent witness to the flaring tension in his jaw. "Why did you stop?" she asked finally, shakily.

"I never should have started."

"But why? I don't understand. I wanted you to go on. I wanted you to make love to me. I *asked* you to."

He held her away then, staring at her oddly.

Edwina looked at him, confused, her breathing shallow. And then she saw the angry marks her fingernails had left on his arms. She was astonished at what she'd done and instantly ashamed.

"I'm sorry," she said in a horrified whisper. She tried to twist away, but he wouldn't let her.

"I'm not." He drew her around to face him. "I'm not, Edwina. You were beautiful and damn sexy."

"I went crazy"—her voice was soft with disbelief —"is that it? Is that why you wouldn't make love to me?"

"*No*—hell, no. I wanted to make love to you, Princess. I still do. I can't think of anything I want more at the moment."

"Then what is it?"

His fingers were sweetly rigid against the curve of her jaw. "It's not easy to explain. You're a kid, really. No, wait—hear me out," he said as she pulled away. "I'm not talking about age, I'm talking about experience. You're looking for something, Ed, and don't deny it. Danger, thrills, a walk on the wild side. You want to discover the 'other' Edwina Moody, but you're afraid of what's there. So you're waiting for it to happen, for someone to make it happen."

"To make what happen?"

"The escape hatch, Alice's mirror, the way to Wonderland—anything that would let you get outside yourself and—"

"And what?" She dared him to say it.

"Be sexy and unashamed," he explained, "the 'other' Edwina. Your whole life you've been waiting for the moment, for the man."

"And you're not the man?"

"I could be."

"But this is not the moment?"

"No, it's not."

She reddened again, a scarlet flush that was beautiful against her fair skin. He knew he could have her—now, if he wanted—tonight, tomorrow, whenever he wanted. She was that susceptible, that deprived of physical gratification. He'd seen the type before. If he was right about her, she'd probably spent a lifetime denying her own needs in favor of others, a lifetime of self-sacrifice. The attraction between them might even be the first glimpse she'd

had of something for *herself*, all for herself. Her
family wouldn't approve, of course, and that would
make it an act of rebellion, a break from the past.
Exactly what she wanted, even if she didn't know it
yet.

"It's okay, Princess," he said, touching her cheek,
testing its downy softness. He wanted to be that
man, the one who could set her free. But he didn't
know how without hurting her. And he would hurt
her. Women like Edwina Moody were born to be hurt
by men who didn't have names, men who tore up
the asphalt and went wherever the next turn in the
road took them. Men who couldn't love anything but
their own freedom.

She nuzzled into his hand like a kitten who wanted
to be caressed. Diablo felt the hard clutch of desire
in his groin. He wouldn't make love to her. He couldn't
take her this way, not and live with himself. But
how the hell did he stop? She was so needy for
everything a man could give her. And he wasn't in a
whole lot better condition himself. Lord, he'd been
without *so damn long*.

She pressed her mouth to his fingers and closed
her eyes, an irresistibly aroused woman.

"We've got a deal," he said, jaw muscles knotting.

She looked at him, limpid-eyed. "I don't care about
that."

"I do. I can't afford to have you asking questions,
hassling the Warlords, almost getting us kicked out
again."

"I won't." She stood back from him, her voice
tightening. "I can handle myself."

He purposely let his eyes drift to her breasts and
linger there. "You couldn't prove that by me, Ed."

Edwina slept by the fire that night. She refused
the sleeping bag, even when Diablo offered to let her
have it all to herself. Finally he zipped the bags
apart, and they slept on opposite sides of the smoldering coals.

Dreams flitted through Edwina's mind, subliminal flashes that left her exhausted because they were so hauntingly real. She tossed fitfully, unable to release herself from the explicit fantasies or from the yearnings that ached through her body.

The first light of dawn awoke her. The dew was still thick on the ground, and it was much too chilly to leave the sleeping bag, so she curled up for warmth and contemplated the man across the campsite from her. Mr. Easy Rider slept on, oblivious to her wakefulness, and Edwina wanted to thump him for it.

His speech from the night before resonated in her mind. She could have recited it word for word. It wasn't so much that he'd done the 'right thing'. A part of her had always known that he was more complicated than he pretended. It was his sensitivity that had surprised her. A hell-for-leather biker with a conscience, she thought ruefully. Maybe even a streak of nobility.

She sighed, bemused, as she thought about what his sudden nobility had done to her. Her body was still thrumming with unrequited urges. She ought to have been worrying about what they'd done last night. Instead, she was obsessed with what they *hadn't* done. He'd given her an irresistible taste of the drugging pleasure he could bring her, and then he'd cut her off. Just enough to get good and hooked, she thought, sighing.

She could only imagine what his nobility must have cost *him*. It had to be agonizing for a man to reach a state of total physical arousal and not act on it. And he had reached that state with her, several times. She'd felt the physical proof of it. What she didn't understand was why he fought it.

He shifted in the sleeping bag, his hair falling across his face as he turned toward her. He was a mystery, she thought, and mysteries had always attracted her. There were occasions when she had watched him grow silent and distant, as though drifting somewhere else, an unmoored boat. She wondered where he went when his eyes were far away. . . .

"Welcome to the living," she said when he finally roused. She had coffee on by then, and he nodded when she lifted the blackened aluminum pot and offered him some.

He'd dragged himself out of the sleeping bag by the time she'd poured the coffee. As she walked toward him, he raised his head and absently raked a hand through the dark hair dusting his chest. He was still half asleep, drowsy and tousled, wearing only jeans. He looked sexy and adorable, dammit, she thought, handing him the coffee. An errant nerve ending ticked in the cleft between her breasts.

"Saved my life," he said, taking the cup. His voice was husky, hoarsened by residues of sleep.

Their fingers brushed briefly, and Edwina felt a thrill that was sharp and galvanizing, nearly as intense as those the night before. She stepped back, fully aware that to be anywhere near him was to risk a sexual response. Since last night her body had become a barometer where he was concerned, exquisitely calibrated, sensitive to every hairbreadth change in his mood.

"I'm going to wash up." She turned away from his curious gaze and headed for the river, aware of his eyes on her. She hoped the sight of her departing backside was giving him half as much grief as he'd been giving her.

She needn't have worried. Diablo felt as though someone had kneed him viciously in the groin as he watched her walk away. A reaction that was the legacy of last night's encounter, he knew. Another bout with her like that one, and he'd be in the emergency room.

"Not a chance," he said aloud. He damn well wasn't going to make love to her, no matter how incredible it promised to be. He wasn't in the business of providing stud service for repressed females. He finished off his coffee in two gulps, conveniently ignoring the complexity of the woman he was dealing with. Frustration had a way of driving a man to simplistic answers, but somewhere in the back of Diablo's mind he knew that if Edwina Moody was repressed, she was also an erotic time bomb, and things were going to get a lot more complicated before they got simple.

"How about some breakfast?" she said, coming up behind him.

He turned and stared hard at her curly blond hair, sweet face, and lithe figure. Why the hell had he ever told her to cut those jeans so short? And that top? She was half *naked,* for chrissake. "That's your job, woman," he said brusquely. "Get cooking. Make me some bacon and eggs."

"Yes, *sir.*" Edwina felt a crackle of anger, and at the same time a flush of something hot and forbidden. For one crazy second she wanted to walk straight over to the arrogant SOB, unsnap his pants, and arouse him in all the ways a woman can arouse a man. She wanted to make him tremble and lose control the way she had . . .

The flush spread like wildfire, stinging her throat. She couldn't believe the things she was thinking! She had sex on the brain, even when she was angry. She had to get herself under control. *Had* to. It was a matter of survival.

Something told her that if she ever succumbed and made love with him, she would simply melt to his will from that day forward. She would lose every shred of autonomy and dissolve into a puddle of desire whenever he crooked his finger. Edwina Jean Moody couldn't imagine herself a slave to anything . . . except him.

"Got a stock tip for me?" Edwina spoke to the back pockets of Killer's jeans. He was bent over his motorcycle, a wrench clutched in his greasy hand, and he looked every inch a grungy gung ho biker. So much so that she wondered if she had imagined him with the *Wall Street Journal* yesterday.

"That is what you're doing, isn't it?" she said. "Playing the stock market?"

Killer craned his neck around and frowned at her. "Nope. I'm wrenching on my scooter."

"Oh, of course." Edwina shrugged carelessly. "I didn't mean now. I meant in general. You do play the market?"

He rose and tipped his L.A. Raiders hat back on his forehead. "I don't play the market—I murder it," he said, squinting into the sun. "That's why they call me Killer."

"Murder the market?" She laughed appreciatively. "Did you learn that in college?"

Killer threw her a funny look and went back to wrenching. "What makes you think I went to college?"

"No reason." Edwina suspected she'd hit a nerve, and it made her even more determined to get some answers. She was going to take a risk, she decided, studying him, a calculated risk. She didn't have the rubber snake with her, but if she could surprise Killer with the picture of Holt and get a reaction out of him, she just might hit the jackpot.

She glanced around, checking out the near-deserted campsite. Most of the gang had headed into town for supplies, including Diablo. They'd been gone a couple of hours, and they could show up at any time.

She dug the picture from her pocket and frowned. It was much the worse for having been in the river with her and Diablo last night. "Got a minute?" she asked Killer's back.

He craned around again and squinted at her, then glanced at the picture as she held it out.

"Anybody you know?" she asked.

"You yanking my chain?"

He looked so incredulous that Edwina's heart began to pound. "Why? *Do* you know him?"

"Hard to tell," he said with a disdainful snick of laughter. "Is this before or after?"

"I was hoping you could tell me."

He straightened up, looked Edwina over suspiciously, then took the photograph out of her hand and gave it another quick hard glance. "I don't know what you're talking about, lady. I never saw this kid before."

The roar of approaching motorcycles warned Edwina that her time had run out. She whisked the picture from Killer's hand and jammed it into her pocket, turning in time to see Squire roll in, Carmen seated behind him.

Diablo trailed at the back of the pack, wearing mirrored sunglasses and the red bandanna around his head. He gunned his bike and roared up beside Edwina, the dust flying. "What are you doing?" he said, his glare flicking from her to Killer.

"Having a conversation." She flagged the dust away with her hand. "Is that against the rules?"

"Get your butt on the bike, woman."

The undisguised hostility in his voice made Edwina bridle. Somehow she managed to keep her mouth shut under the penetrating stares of the Warlords, but her heart burned with outrage. Silent, furious, she climbed on the bike and crossed her arms, refusing to touch him as he sped off toward their camp.

The second he pulled into their campsite, she slid off and glowered at him. "Don't ever do that to me again," she said. "I don't care what our deal is. I don't care how the Warlords treat their women. If you ever humiliate me like that again, I'll—"

"You'll what?" He swung off the machine, hit the kickstand, and loomed over her.

"I'll beat you to a bloody pulp with your own bike chain."

A smile flickered. "That tough, huh?"

The threat had been a bit more graphic than Edwina intended, but she stood by it. "That tough."

"The rodeo starts day after tomorrow," he said. "You and I have got forty-eight more hours to get through, and we're *going* to get through it."

Edwina returned his stare defiantly, holding her ground, daring him to cross the symbolic line she'd drawn. He snagged her wrist and jerked her toward him, staring down at her until she felt herself weakening. She held her breath as his eyes flared, rich and emerald green. Seconds flew by, quick silent beats that connected them in some frightening way she didn't fully understand.

"We're going to do this my way, Princess," he said, bringing her face up as though he were going to kiss her. And then Edwina realized that he *was* going to kiss her. His eyes had gone black with desire, and she could almost feel the stirring of his breath on her lips.

She rose up, trembling, lifting her mouth to his. Their lips touched, and she'd barely closed her eyes before he caught hold of her arms. A violent curse shook on his breath as he wrenched himself back from her. His voice dropped low, the same hair-raising whisper she remembered from Blackie's.

"We're going to do this my way," he said. "*Or we're not going to do it at all.*"

Six

Diablo's "way" turned out to be the ultimate test of Edwina's patience. For the next two days he put an entirely new spin on the word *tension*. He was brusque and remote. He barked out commands like a marine DI, even going so far as to suggest that Edwina wash and wax his bike as the other old ladies did.

"Got some mud on those rims," he announced late the following afternoon as he pulled a beer from the six-pack he had cooling in the river. He settled back against a bigleaf maple, popped the top, and took a swig. He'd barely lowered his arm and wiped his mouth before he was pointing Edwina toward the mud-spattered bike. "Spokes could use some elbow grease too."

Edwina drew the line at that. "I don't *do* spokes," she told him flatly. "However, I'd be happy to run the bike into the river if you'd like, spokes and all."

He took a deep pull from the beer can, flashed her a scowl, and then settled his gaze on the river.

A prince, she thought, I've finally found my prince. She shot visual daggers at his handsome, sullen profile. The bike first and then you, Mr. Congeniality. And may you both sink to the bottom like cement blocks.

She began busying herself with dinner, a mess of

catfish the men had caught that morning. The rodeo started the next day, she reminded herself, striking a match to the logs left over from last night's fire. She would have another shot at Killer then, and even if Killer wasn't Holt, the real item was sure to turn up. Earlier that day Carmen had told her the rodeo was the biggest motorcycling event of the summer. Not only were they expecting several thousand "brothers" from all over the country, but it was going to be televised by a national network.

Moments later, as she settled the frying pan on its makeshift grate over the low-burning coals, she glanced at Diablo again. Contemplating his dark surliness, she marveled at the power of the attraction she felt for him, despite everything. Part of it was purely physical, she knew. *Handsome* didn't begin to do him justice. The cheekbones, the eyelashes— God. She could thank her lucky stars that he was also unbearably nasty. She wouldn't have been able to keep her hands off him otherwise. She was having trouble as it was.

He tilted his head against the tree, and the flashing light from the river outlined his three-quarter profile in silver. It was a reflective pose, and Edwina found it impossible not to wonder what he was thinking about. Past lives? Lost loves?

She slapped the catfish in the frying pan. If he was thinking about anything at all, she decided, it was probably riding motorcycles and ordering women around.

He had been acting oddly though, she admitted, even beyond his surliness toward her. The camp had been deserted the day before while the Warlords were swimming, and she'd noticed Diablo moving through the empty campsites. At one point she thought she'd seen him going through someone's saddlebags, but when she asked him about it, he'd claimed he was doing some repair work on the bike. "A favor for a brother," he'd said, so abruptly, she'd let the matter go. The last thing she'd needed then—or now—was to provoke him any further. She hadn't bought his story, though, not entirely. Whatever his reasons for joining the gang, she was beginning to suspect they weren't limited to brotherhood and fast bikes.

Much later that night as she lay in her sleeping bag staring at the stars, Edwina was quite sure she was losing whatever grip she had left on reality. She'd been listening to crickets for hours, until suddenly another sound caught her attention. Soft and plaintive as a songbird's call, it came from the distance, perhaps even from the vicinity of the main camp. What kind of bird would make that sound? she wondered, trying to follow the melody. It actually sounded a little like "Kumbaya, My Lord," an African folk song she vaguely recollected from summer camp when she was a kid.

It was only as Edwina began to hum along that she realized it wasn't a bird at all. It was a harmonica! A quick glance at Diablo told her he wasn't sleeping either, which meant that she would have to postpone any immediate investigating. She smiled up at the star-strewn sky. A Warlord who played the harmonica. Now, that was interesting.

Rodeos. Edwina hadn't been to more than one or two such events in all of her twenty-six years. She was an easterner to the bone, but she'd always fondly associated rodeos with bucking horses, sweaty Stetsons, and kids shoveling cow pies off stable floors. A bikers' rodeo, however, was quite a different kettle of soup, she was learning.

For one thing, there was the constant thunder of motorcycles—choppers, screamin' eagles, and monster machines of every variety varooming into the fairgrounds. The men piloting the bikes were straight out of *Easy Rider*—highway commandos, tough-talking scrappers, and rugged individualists all. The women perched behind them had attitude to spare. They were street savvy and supercool. If there was a

dress code, Edwina realized, it was tight jeans, tattoos, and leather. For both men and women.

Edwina was awestruck by the gaudy spectacle and
had to remind herself not to stare. She felt as though
she'd walked through the looking glass Diablo had
said she was searching for. It was certainly a different world, a freewheeling subculture that most people probably didn't know existed. Fascinated, she
walked around the grounds, browsing at souvenir
booths that featured such diverse items as custom
wheelcovers, silver slave bracelets, and solid-brass
skulls.

Later she stopped to watch a trick-riding demo
and contemplate a banner hanging over the hot-dog-
and-beer concession: FLYING WHEELS RODEO: LET
THE GOOD TIMES ROLL!

Finally Edwina had to remind herself that she had
more important things to do than soak up the ambi-
ence. Diablo was competing in the barrel-racing event,
and she needed to accomplish several things while
he was occupied. In addition to scouting the fairgrounds for men who matched Holt's physical description, she intended to track down Killer and ask
a few more friendly questions. She also had a harmonica player to locate, but since he was obviously a
Warlord, that could wait.

Black leather, long hair, and Rip Van Winkle beards
seemed to be the order of the day as Edwina scoured
the fairgrounds. She might as well have been at a
Halloween party where everyone was wearing the
same costume. Not a talkative bunch either, she
realized after numerous abortive attempts at conversation. More often than not her questions were de-
flected with monosyllabic responses that sounded
more like grunts than words. It wasn't until she
began to pepper her small talk with references to
camshafts, flywheels, and air cleaners that she gar-
nered some grudging respect. But no leads.

At one point she noticed Mad Dog in furtive conversation with a short stocky man in a trench coat.
She stopped for a moment to watch, curious as a

flash of light drew her attention to the chrome object ticked in Mad Dog's boot. She still couldn't tell what it was, and after a moment she shook off the fascination. She had better things to do.

Edwina was thoroughly tired and discouraged by the time she came across Killer at a tattoo booth. Stranded on a campstool, he was undergoing the ministrations of a female tattoo artist named Mother Earth according to the booth's sign.

A captive audience, Edwina thought, smiling to herself. What luck! She reminded herself to play it cool as she approached him, but her attention was instantly riveted by the coiled python the artist was wrapping around Killer's upper arm. The caption underneath it advised the reader to watch his step, but in less polite language.

"My goodness," Edwina breathed. It was not the sort of thing a man who was afraid of snakes would choose, she realized. Unless he was trying to prove something.

Killer grinned at her. "Like it?"

"It's lovel—" She caught herself. "Bad, Killer. That's one *bad* snake."

"Thanks," he said, nodding toward the flaming skull on her shoulder. "Yours is pretty gnarly, too."

"Oh, this . . ." She shrugged it off. "I'm going to get myself a boa constrictor just as soon as I can scrape up the bread."

He considered her with renewed respect.

Progress. Intuition told Edwina to take it slowly, but she had so little time. "Killer, you look like a man who knows his way around."

Maneuvering clear of the bulky girth of the tattoo artist, Edwina crouched beside Killer's stool and spoke in conspiratorial whispers. "If I wanted to make contact with a guy—one of the brothers, I mean—how would I do that? I was told he'd be here, at the rodeo."

He looked her over. "You the fuzz?"

"No—this has nothing to do with the police." She tried another angle—the bearer-of-good-news technique. "I've got some information for him I think he'll want to hear."

"Yeah? So what's his name?"

She paused for effect. "Christopher Holt."

Killer scratched his scruffy beard and studied her through narrowing eyes. "If I did know something about this Holt dude," he said, "what would it be worth to you?"

"Ed!"

Edwina turned to see Carmen waving her arms and rushing toward them from the stadium area.

"We'll talk later," she assured Killer under her breath, hastily abandoning him to the tattoo artist.

Laughing and breathless, Carmen blurted out the news the minute she reached Edwina. "You and Diablo are entered in the pig-roping competition," she said. "Hurry! It's up next."

"Pig roping?" Edwina resisted, digging in her heels as Carmen tried to tug her along. "Is that what it sounds like? Who signed us up?"

"Squire did it." Carmen's dark eyes sparked in the sunlight. "Get a hustle on, Ed. If you and Diablo want to be in the Warlords, you'd better bring home the bacon!"

Edwina had very dark thoughts on her mind as Carmen dragged her toward the stadium. Her first glimpse of Diablo told her that he wasn't any happier about the situation than she was. He was standing near the announcer's booth talking to Squire, and he looked as though he were losing the argument.

Diablo pulled Edwina aside as she approached. Behind them the stadium crowd roared with laughter at something going on in the arena. "Looks like we're stuck with this pig-roping thing," he said. "Ever thrown a lasso?"

"Once, at a Junior League charity bazaar. I swung it over my head pretty good, but then I looked up and got dizzy." She smiled faintly. "I sort of lassoed myself."

He closed his eyes. "Worse than I thought."

While they waited for their turn, Diablo gave Edwina some pointers, but he might as well have been trying to teach her quantum physics. She did master the rules, however. The event required that the man maneuver the bike while the woman wielded the lasso. Each pair had two minutes in the arena with the pig, and the team with the best time won.

The crowd was still roaring as Edwina and Diablo took their positions on his bike. They were slotted as the last team to compete, and as Edwina watched the couples before them chase the pig around, tormenting the poor squealing creature on their motorcycles, she became incensed. The pathetic animal would probably die of a heart attack before anyone got a rope on it. Her only consolation was that the pig seemed to be giving the contestants a run for their money. It dodged and darted, maneuvering like greased lightning.

"Let's hear it for the bacon busters!" the MC yelled, stirring up the crowd. "I'm going to throw in a bonus," he said. "The winners get to take Porky home! Barbecued spareribs tonight!"

Edwina winced as the pig was finally lassoed and brought to a screeching halt. Spareribs indeed, she thought.

She thumped Diablo on the back. "We've got to win this event," she said, her voice shaking with conviction. "I refuse to let any of these bozos take that poor creature home and barbecue him."

Diablo was incredulous. "What are we going to do with a pig?"

Edwina had no answer for that. Furthermore, she found the question irrelevant. The pig needed rescuing, and she was the only one who cared, quite obviously.

Diablo cranked around and gave her a hard stare. In the face of her unflinching passion, he exhaled. "All right, you want the pig, you got it."

A prince, Edwina thought, smiling.

Moments later, in the middle of the arena, waiting for the pig to be released, Edwina was no longer smiling. The crowd whistled and stomped as the animal came scrambling out of the chute. Diablo gassed the bike, and they were off. She clamped her thighs tight to his hips, which left both of her hands free to work the rope.

"Now!" Diablo said as he pulled alongside the galloping pig. Edwina rose out of her seat, swinging the rope awkwardly. The pig swerved. Diablo swerved with it, and Edwina dug her knees into his body for leverage. She leaned over him, swaying precariously. The pig pulled ahead, and as Diablo shot out after it, Edwina let fly with the lasso. By some miracle, her aim was on target.

"She's got it!" someone screamed.

"Oh, no!" A groan went up as the rope hit the pig's snout and bounced off.

"One more time," Diablo said, spinning the bike around. "This time we bag him," he told Edwina. "Let me get close. Stay low and lay the loop over his head."

Edwina's obsession with liberating the pig made her reckless. As Diablo pulled up on the animal, she dipped down low enough to stir up dust with the loop of the rope. It was a dicey maneuver for an inexperienced rider, and the crowd gasped.

What happened next was one of those unforseen incidents that change the course of events inexorably. It would live on in biker folklore for years to come that Diablo's cycle fishtailed into a one-eighty spinout just as the pig changed direction. It might have been Edwina's weight or even a wet spot on the dirt field. Whatever the reason, for several horrible seconds before Diablo could get the bike under control, motorcycle and pig were on a collision course.

When the animal saw them coming at him, he put on the brakes and squealed in confusion. As Diablo and Edwina rolled by, the pig simply sat back on its haunches, spent. Edwina gently dropped the lasso over its head.

The crowd went crazy.

"A big hand for our winners!" the MC trumpeted moments later as Edwina and Diablo climbed the stairs to the awards podium. Television cameras whirred as the MC held out a large silver trophy and clapped Diablo soundly on the back.

"Give your old lady a kiss!" he urged. "She's one tough little pig wrangler!"

"She is that," Diablo admitted.

Edwina couldn't suppress a smile. By the expression on Diablo's face, the last thing he wanted to do at the moment was kiss her.

She was partially right. Actually Diablo wanted to kiss the hell out of her. He just didn't want to get anywhere near her sweet little pig-wrangling body to do it. He'd been fighting his animal instincts too long and too hard to risk unleashing the beast again.

"Plant one on her, man!" the MC urged.

Diablo raked a hand through his hair and debated. Edwina looked so breathless and pleased with herself that he found it almost impossible to resist her. Anyway, he rationalized, the TV cameras were rolling. He caught her hand and pulled her to him.

"Good roping, Ed," he said, tilting her chin up. He placed his lips over hers and heard the taut little whimper that came out of her. Good God, he thought, feeling a sharp answering tug deep in his vitals. This woman was going to kill him.

"Good riding," she said, breaking away to touch his jawline with shaky fingers.

He stared into her russet eyes and knew it was too late. His heart was going soft around the edges, and something in the deeper regions of his body was doing exactly the opposite. The beast was free. "Come here, woman," he said, gathering her into his arms. As she melted against him, he kissed her roughly and possessively.

A second later they'd both forgotten all about MCs and stadium crowds and TV cameras. All Diablo could think about was how unbelievably right she felt in his arms.

• • •

The Warlords celebrated that night, a party to end all parties. They congregated at the campsite with Edwina as the guest of honor, and when the gang ragged her about roasting her prize pig with an apple in its mouth, she talked them into adopting it as a mascot instead.

"Let's call him Food Chain," Edwina suggested. "Since that's the fate we saved him from."

The crowd approved. The pig approved, too, apparently. Food Chain wandered happily through the crowd, begging snacks and attention while the Warlords feasted on buckets of fried chicken and biscuits they'd picked up at a fast-food place.

Someone provided hot dogs and marshmallows for roasting over the fire, and for the first time Edwina felt actually a part of the camaraderie. Perhaps Diablo did too. He spent most of the night drinking with the guys, a Warlord ritual, but she noticed him smiling now and then, especially when he caught her eye.

Once or twice in all the commotion Edwina remembered her mission, but Killer wasn't anywhere to be found that night. As the party wore on, it was Mad Dog who drew her attention. He was surprisingly jovial and inoffensive. And when he pulled the wicked-looking silver object from his boot and began to play it, Edwina did a double take. It was a harmonica!

As she hummed along to "Let the Good Times Roll," she realized that Mad Dog must have been the one she'd heard playing the night before. Automatically she touched the front pocket of her jeans where the picture of Chris Holt still languished. Holt had clutched a harmonica, she thought, observing Mad Dog closely. The bearded biker was the right height and the right complexion. He was much too burly, but a man could bulk up in that many years. And she did seem to recall having seen a freckle or two on the biker's nose when he'd tried to molest her in Blackie's.

No, she thought, that's ridiculous. Mad Dog couldn't

be Chris Holt. Vulgarity was a congenital condition with him. He was a roughneck by birth, not a refugee from upper-class stock. Besides, nobody so reprehensible deserved to inherit a fortune. She dismissed the idea and helped herself to one of the deliciously gooey marshmallows Carmen was toasting.

As the celebrating wound down, Squire walked to the roaring fire pit and called the group to attention. "I think the time has come to make Diablo a brother."

A murmur went up among the crowd, and Edwina searched out Diablo with her eyes. He was standing at the edge of the activity, silently observant, and as always, unreadable.

Diablo watched as the club members' heads began to nod. The positive responses told him that his efforts had finally paid off. He was about to become a Warlord. Relief was sharp, a stinging prickle in his gut that surprised him. Not that he didn't have plenty to be relieved about, but it was more than that, he realized. Squire's gesture felt like a personal victory. Aware that Edwina was watching him, he motioned for her to join him.

"Are we going to initiate him?" someone yelled.

"Make him eat a handful of gaskets!" another suggested.

"And drink a quart of transmission fluid," Mad Dog chimed in. Several others hollered their preferred choice of torture as Diablo and Edwina approached Squire.

The gang leader positioned himself in front of the two of them like a country preacher about to perform a ceremony. "Your initiation will be the same as mine when I joined," he said, addressing Diablo, "the Cliff Ride. Will you accept the challenge?"

The crowd began to buzz excitedly, and someone behind Diablo whispered, "The Cliff Ride? That's suicide."

Diablo's jaw tightened. He'd never actually witnessed the Cliff Ride, but he'd heard about its hazards. It was a dangerous stunt that took two people. He glanced at Edwina, at her rising color. Fear? It might have been disbelief in her answering glance or the panic that came with not knowing what to expect. There was only one choice to make, he realized. Squire was giving him the opening he'd been waiting for, but he couldn't subject Edwina to that kind of danger, not even to get into the Warlords.

"I'll accept any challenge but that one," he said, meeting Squire's cold stare head-on. "I don't want my old lady involved."

Edwina looked up at Diablo in surprise, hesitating only as he warned her with a staying motion. His unflinching profile told her there was a great deal at stake. *His* old lady, she thought, as words flashed into her head. The same proprietary phrase that had made her bridle before now gave her an odd rush of pride.

"Do you accept the challenge?" Squire maintained stubbornly. "Yes or no?"

Edwina's heartbeat was erratic as she waited for Diablo to answer. She knew he was trying to protect her. She also knew the initiation was the only way he could gain entrance into the gang. As the silence stretched, she turned to him, took in a strengthening draught of air, and spoke quietly. "Whatever the Cliff Ride is, we can do it. Accept the challenge."

It was midnight when the Warlords convened at Devil Rock. The full moon was a huge white discus resting on black-velvet hills, playing fields of the mountain gods. Once the roar of the cycles had died down, you could almost hear wind whistling through the treetops. The sound of it made Edwina shiver, despite the fact that the air held a late-summer balm.

Disturbed by the intruders to their lair, magnificent red-tailed hawks circled in the night sky, their wings tipped silver by moonlight. The shadows they dropped onto the steep cliff walls of the canyon accentuated the one-hundred-foot drop to the turbulent river below.

Seated behind Diablo on the bike, Edwina felt

nearly ill with fear. She couldn't look at the chasm they were about to negotiate without imagining the horror of plummeting to the bottom. Her mind was torturing her with stark flashes of their bodies broken against the rocks below.

"Are you ready?" Squire asked Diablo.

Diablo nodded, revving the engine of his bike.

Edwina made a silent request of the mountain gods for safe passage. Their challenge was to ride the bike across the twenty-foot natural-rock bridge that connected the two cliffs. Not an impossible task, except that in this case, Diablo was to be blindfolded. Edwina would be his eyes.

It would be a nerve-numbing test of their ability to cooperate, an exercise in trust that was dangerous to the point of insanity. Edwina understood only too well what was at risk: one bad call, one false step on her part, and they were over the side.

Carmen proceeded to untie Diablo's red bandanna and remove it. She then produced a large rectangle of black muslin that she used to blindfold him, knotting it tightly at the back of his head. "Good luck," she whispered, touching Edwina's hand.

Edwina couldn't respond, not even to nod. A part of her psyche had detached, split off completely from the horror of what they were about to do. Another part of her, still rational, couldn't believe that she had ever agreed to such craziness. They were going to die! They were going to plummet into the black chasm of death and cease to exist.

"Sit tight," Diablo told her as he directed the bike toward the granite bridge. "I'm going to gun it."

"Gun it?" Edwina was painfully out of breath. "Why?"

"The momentum will carry us, maybe even give us some lift. If I can't see where I'm going, then the hell with it, I'm going to fly across."

"We, Diablo, *we*. I'm sitting right behind you, and I don't like flying. I can guide you, I promise, just follow my directions." Her fingers tightened on his arm, and the answering contractions of his bicep made her realize that he was as tense as she was.

"I hate to be a bore," he said grimly, "but aren't you the one who opened your mouth and got us into this?"

"I know I got us into this!" she whispered. "Now, please, trust me to get us out of it."

"Trust you," he muttered. "That's rich."

Edwina's heart wrenched painfully as he cranked the throttle and edged the cycle toward the crossing. He stopped the bike several feet from the cliff as though coming to a decision. "How about those directions?" he said abruptly.

"Right! You're fine," she told him. "Straight ahead. Twelve o'clock."

He geared down and started across slowly. "A little to the left now—eleven o'clock," she urged. "Yes! That's good."

She continued calling out directions—and fighting off paralyzing bouts of panic whenever he neared the edge. The rocks were uneven and dangerously slick in places, causing the motorcycle to jolt and slide. Chunks of granite broke loose and tumbled into the chasm as the bike's wheels ground out a precarious traction. As they reached the halfway point, Edwina opened her own fisted hand and saw that she'd drawn blood with her fingernails.

The emotion she felt could be described only as sickening fear. Her breath was trapped in a vise, squashed by the frantic grip of her lungs, and every crackle of sound, every fragment of loose gravel, sent her heart thundering.

"Left! Nine o'clock!" she cried as the bike slid sideways on a slippery piece of rock. "Oh, dear God!" She grabbed for Diablo as they veered toward the edge.

Diablo hit the gas and swung the heavy bike around, fighting desperately to bring it out of the grinding, tire-shredding skid. He was taut as wire, every muscle bulging, every tendon rigid as he heaved and twisted, forced to use gut physical strength to stop the slide. His leg shot out to steady them as the back tire dropped into a groove, and his hands were shaking on the handle grips as he brought the huge machine under control at last.

"You okay?" he asked jagged-voiced.

"Yes—" A hot flare of relief burned through Edwina. Squeezing her eyes shut, she fought down the need to cry and scream and shake. She couldn't let herself fall apart now. She had to get it together. She was his eyes, dammit. And crazy as it seemed, she was his courage too. He took all his signals from her, and if she let him know how precarious it was, how terrifyingly close they'd come to the edge, to death, she would rattle him.

"Straighten it out," she said, barely able to talk. "Let's bring this baby home."

Several more terrifying seconds passed before they reached the other side. As the bike's front wheels touched solid ground, Edwina let out a scream of relief. She threw her arms around Diablo and cried with joy.

"We did it," he said, twisting the throttle.

As he gassed it off the bridge, his back wheel hit some loose ground, and the bike lost traction. Gravel sprayed wildly, and Edwina screamed as she felt the rear end of the machine drop. She grabbed for Diablo, catching hold of his vest as the bike's back wheel spun off the cliff.

Edwina had no strength left. Fear had bled her muscles dry, and it was all she could do to hang on to him as he fought to bring the massive cycle onto safe ground. The bike vibrated violently, shrieking its primacy over nature, and her world exploded in roaring engines and flying, splintering rock.

In the next savage burst of effort Diablo manually inched the bike toward safety, and they finally burst free, hurtling onto solid land. He hit the brakes, ripped off his blindfold, and roared with triumph. Edwina collapsed against the sissy bar, too weak even to express her relief.

Somewhere in the distance she heard the Warlords yelling and cheering, and then she felt Diablo's arms around her and knew she was being lifted from the bike.

Through a blur of exhaustion she saw Squire coming across the bridge toward them. The older man rushed at Diablo, caught him around the shoulders, and bear-hugged him.

"You're a Warlord, man," Squire said, presenting Diablo with the red bandanna, now an official symbol of his membership.

Diablo exhaled a gust of harsh laughter. He handed Squire the black blindfold, and the Warlords shouted their approval.

"There is one last thing, Brother," Squire told Diablo as he nodded toward Edwina. "It's her turn now. You know the rules."

Edwina roused herself long enough to peer at both of the men. "*Her* turn?"

Diablo's shoulders stiffened as he faced the Warlord's leader. "I know the rules, Squire, but she's my old lady. I initiate her in my own way."

Seven

Diablo's motorcycle sped through the deep canyon, passing foliage and boulders that could barely be seen in the thin streams of moonlight reflecting off the walls. The bike and its riders were dwarfed by the majesty that surrounded them—white-faced cliffs and hoary outcroppings that resembled ancient gargoyles in Gothic architecture. The canyon was the wild heart of the mountains, frighteningly beautiful.

Diablo banked into a sudden curve, and Edwina touched his indrawn arm, her body swaying into him naturally. The warmth of his skin startled her, and she drew back involuntarily. Everything felt charged and spiky between them now, she realized. Even accidental touches were made premonitory by a sense of something about to happen.

"Where are we going?" she called to him. All he had told her was that the rite of initiation wasn't over.

"Up ahead," he called back.

The canyon opened up onto an amphitheater of living rock—smooth sleek granite, jagged slate, and ribbed limestone. Diablo headed for an opening in the cliffs in front of them, a dark, yawning maw that looked endless, as though it might connect the mountain with an alternative universe.

"It looks like a cave," she said. "Why are we going there?"

"Hang on. You'll see."

She felt zephyrs of cool air caress her face as they cruised into the mouth of the tunnel. The engine's soft rumble ricocheted off the walls, and almost instantly they were swimming in a darkness so total it felt like deep-sea water. Edwina's field of vision was obliterated. Disorientation swept her and she clutched Diablo, thankful for his reassuring warmth.

It seemed to her that they'd been riding forever, and then a sound came to her from far away. It was silvery and melodious, like tinsel rustling in the wind or the shimmer of harpstrings. The darkness above them sparkled with an eerie phosphorescence, and Edwina had the feeling she was staring up at open sky, at stardust and infinity.

A shaft of light burst out of nowhere. Edwina inhaled sharply as more and more light poured through the darkness until the path before them was illuminated with pearlescence. The rustling sound became a breathtaking roar. Before she knew what was happening, the wall alongside them had dissolved in the thunder of a waterfall. A fine spray coated Edwina's arms and face as Diablo drove past cautiously.

"The grotto," he said a moment later as they rolled into an open-air fairyland. Exotic ferns hung from jutting rocks, and a pair of waterfalls oozed from crevices between the boulders and spilled into a lagoonlike pool. Edwina looked up and saw that the stardust above them was the real thing. The sky was studded with constellations.

"This is breathtaking," she said, aware that Diablo had slid off the bike and was waiting for her. She spent the next several moments admiring the grotto, remarking on the lush greenery and the sparkling pool that bubbled up like warm champagne. Was it fed by an underground hot springs? she wondered. Did the cavern date back to prehistoric times? Drinking in the scent of honeysuckle, she gazed up at the starry night until she was dizzy. And all the while, the question that loomed large in her mind was *what next*?

A sparkle of curious humor lit Diablo's eyes. "Are you planning on getting off the bike anytime soon?" he asked.

"Well . . . sure."

She took his outstretched hand, aware that she was not only alone with him but more isolated from the world than she'd ever been with a man. She'd already sensed what this part of the ritual involved, but she didn't want to ask and have her fears confirmed. The irony of that reticence didn't escape her. During their kiss at the stadium, she would have sold Food Chain to a meat-packer for some time alone with Diablo. Now that she had both the time and the opportunity, she was losing her nerve again.

"I guess we're not here for a picnic," she said softly.

Diablo agreed with a shrug. "Not unless you brought some fried chicken."

"Cluck, cluck," Edwina murmured.

"Nothing has to happen, Ed," he said finally. "Not unless you want it to."

She plucked at a blond curl that had wandered onto her cheek. "If I did want it to, what would *it* be?"

Diablo studied her flushed expectancy, beguiled by the unconscious innocence she projected. She was irresistible. She made him feel dangerously male, both predator and protector. She made him feel tender and carnal. He wanted her body like hell on fire, and now that he was a Warlord, there was nothing to stop him. Nothing but her. The initiation he chose for her had to be right. Slow and sweet. Sexy and mind-blowing.

"Have you ever heard of the Maiden's Spring?" he said.

She thought a moment. "It comes from mythology, doesn't it?"

"Close. It's a Celtic legend about a timber wolf who wanted to make love to a woman." He walked to the waterfall and held out his hand, letting the water splash through his fingers. "According to the legend, the wolf led the woman to the Maiden's Spring, and when she drank its charmed water, he took human form."

Human form, Edwina thought, drawn to Diablo's dark hair and mesmerizing green eyes. "And did he make love to her then?"

"No, he couldn't. She had released his body from animal form, but not his spirit. The woman could see he was in agony, and she began to cry. The wolf gave her a wildflower for her hair and told her to bathe in the pool and wash her tears away."

"And did she?"

He nodded. "Afterward, she took the flower from her hair and set it adrift on the water. The flower was a larkspur. It symbolized freedom."

"And that released him?"

"Yes . . . and then they made love."

Edwina felt warmth radiate up her throat. Her heart was a little crazy, but she actually thought the legend was rather lovely. "And that would be my initiation?"

"Yes . . . there's just one other thing you ought to know, Ed. When the woman released the wolf, she gave up her right to refuse him."

"Refuse him what?"

"Anything he asked."

His eyes darkened as he said the words, and Edwina's heart went completely crazy. "Anything he asks? *Anything?*" She stepped back from him.

"That's the legend, Princess."

Edwina's breathing sharpened painfully as she thought about what he was asking of her. She brought a hand to her throat, drawing together the neckline of her top. The cave suddenly felt chilly and alien. "I'm not sure I can do that."

"Do you *want* to do it?"

Edwina's heartbeat went thready as he approached her. It was happening to her again, she realized, the same bizarre physical reaction she'd had at the reflecting pool. She felt strange, loose at the joints, and dizzy, as though the mountain air were affecting her equilibrium.

Diablo touched her forearm, and the heat of his skin shocked her. She pulled back and felt him respond with a staying hold, engulfing slender bones in his grasp. Edwina blinked down at his hand, at the facile strength of his fingers and the bronzed hues of his skin. The sight of him holding her and the unexpected contact of their skin set her imagination on fire.

She remembered his hands spanning her waist, cupping her breasts, and deep inside she felt a clutch of something that could only be desire. It shivered through her like restless water. It gripped and caressed her tender parts like seeking fingers. Edwina resisted the sensation, her stomach muscles tightening. Too fast, she thought. It was happening too fast. That was what frightened her about being with him. Her responses were lightning quick. One touch and she was liquid.

He'd aroused her to a state of near agony that night in the pool. He'd slipped his leg between hers and driven her half mad with ecstasy. And now it was happening again.

"Are you all right, Ed?"

He drew his finger along the inside of her wrist, a gentle stroking gesture probably meant to reassure. Instead it inflamed. The sensitive area was an erogenous zone for Edwina, her own personal weakness of the flesh. A whimper locked in her throat, and it was then that the truth of her frantic responses hit her. Maybe it wasn't sex on the brain. Maybe it was just plain womanly need. The need to be physical with a man, to be held and caressed, to feel his hard muscles and harder bones pressing into the tender parts of her body.

Heat seeped up the crevice between Edwina's shoulder blades and warmed her neck. Maybe it was need, dammit, she thought. Otherwise, she didn't know what the hell was wrong with her. Or why she was swearing, for that matter. She *never* swore at home.

"Tell me what you want, Princess."

His voice was gentle. It was husky and rich with

male sexual ardor. Edwina felt herself melting inside. "Princess." She turned to syrup when he talked like that, called her that. If she had any willpower left, what she ought to do was leave. Quickly. Escape before his caresses had bled off all her control. Escape before he did something outrageous. And *she* liked it!

Her emotions whipsawed between flight and fantasy. If she stayed, she would certainly discover the "other" Edwina Moody he'd talked about. She might even learn things about herself that she didn't want to know. But if she left, she knew she would regret it forever, wonder forever what might have happened.

"All that Maiden's-Spring stuff?" she said. "Is it absolutely necessary?"

He brought her chin up. "Nothing's necessary, Ed."

The moonlight danced shadows over his features, and Edwina was caught off guard by his masculine beauty. His bones seemed carved out of the darkness, the lines of his face rapaciously gaunt. Long black hair gleamed in the starlight. El Diablo, she thought . . . the devil.

"What are you doing to me?" Her voice was as whispery as the water cascading behind them.

"Nothing . . . yet."

"You know what I mean. I'm not the kind of woman who whimpers and melts all over the place. It's not my style, this drowning-in-passion stuff. So what are you doing?"

"I think you're doing it, Ed. Give yourself credit."

She drew away from him, away from the dreamy stroking of his finger on her wrist. "I don't want credit."

"What are you afraid of?"

"That's easy. You."

"What do you think I'm going to do to you?"

"I don't know. All kind of things . . . everything."

"I will if you want."

She couldn't take her eyes from him. She was transfixed by his shadowed features, caught in a way that she knew would haunt her dreams forever. She would close her eyes tonight—and every night— and see emerald eyes, black-lashed and piercing, set like gemstones in an outlaw's handsome face. She couldn't tell him what she wanted. It was scorchingly sensual, what she wanted. It was torrid.

"Maybe a rain check?" she said.

Edwina watched, fascinated as he wet his lips with his tongue, quickly, imperceptibly. It made her think of the time that she had touched her own lips . . . and he'd become aroused just watching her. Remembering, she did it again, touching herself with unsteady fingers, thrilling to the naked sensitivity.

"Don't do that, Princess," he said. "Not unless you want a wild man on your hands."

Edwina's heart quickened. And yet she continued, drawing her forefinger slowly along the width of her lips, and watching his eyes go smoky. She could hardly believe her own recklessness. She was actually trying to entice him. It had to be the most dangerous thing she'd ever done!

His hand cinched her wrist, and he whipped her forward so abruptly that she lost her balance and fell into his arms.

"Don't say you didn't ask for this," he said, his mouth closing over hers roughly. He clamped a hand to her behind, palming her intimately as he brought her up against his lower body. She could feel him growing hard as he held her, tautening against her body. It was frightening and thrilling to feel every inch of him so explicitly. A whimper rose in Edwina's throat.

He deepened the kiss, crushing her lips under his. His free hand curved to the heavy ache of her breast, as though he could touch her anywhere he wanted, take any liberties with her body he chose. Edwina knew she had to stop him, but the riot of sensation inside her was shattering her control. The kiss was hot and hard and sexy, its message clear. He was a Warlord, and a Warlord took what he wanted when he wanted it. He massaged her breast in rhythm with the deep movements of his mouth, roughing her up a little before he let go of her, his eyes blazing.

"Is that what you wanted?" he asked.

She shook her head, her heart throbbing painfully. Her lips tingled with the shock of what he'd done. "That was unbelievably crude. Why did you do it?"

"Because *I'm* crude." *And because you did want it,* his expression told her. The fire in his eyes banked a little as he considered her indignant distress. "Don't play games with me, Ed," he said, his voice lowering. "I know them all. I've been playing them a lot longer than you have."

Edwina turned away from him, still breathless, still angry.

She heard him walk to his bike and hit the kickstand. "What are you doing?" she asked, turning.

"I assumed you'd want to leave."

He could leave just like that? Unaffected? When she was shaking from head to toe? The arrogance, she thought, wishing she had a withering comeback. Anything to shake him up a little. "Don't you ever lose control?"

Laughter sparkled in his eyes. "I think I just did."

"No, I mean really lose control, the way I do . . ."

He was suddenly alert, and faintly predatory. "How *do* you lose control?" He left the bike and walked toward her.

The words spilled out of her haltingly. "I fall apart when you touch me. I have these warm, watery feelings inside that make me think I'm drowning."

He stood in front of her, and touching only her cheek, he bent over her and kissed her gently, a delicious drifting of warm breath across her waiting lips.

Afterward, he curved his hands to her face. "Drink from the spring with me, Princess, and let me show you how good those feelings can be, how wild and sweet and tender."

As he stared into her eyes, Edwina had the feeling of being probed, gently and deliberately penetrated.

It left her weak with need. He could do that so effortlessly, she realized, reach inside her with a look and draw up sensations that made her feel as though she were dying of need.

She let herself be led to the waterfall.

Cupping his hands, he filled them with foaming bubbles that instantly resolved into crystal-clear water. He drank slowly of the water, and then, droplets still clinging to his lips, he offered some to her.

She moved to him, gazing at her own reflection in the glistening water. Her eyes were amber liquid, swimming in the golden fringe of her lashes. Drawn to her own likeness, she touched her lips to the coolness and at the same time felt the heel of his palm brush against her cheek. Her reflection shimmered and disappeared as she sipped, and she had the oddest sensation of drinking of herself. The water swirled and flowed down her throat, strangely effervescent.

Diablo let the remaining water spill to the ground. He touched wet fingers to her throat, a smile curving his lips. "Let's initiate you, Princess."

"Initiate . . ." Her heart went crazy. "Now?"

"Yes."

Edwina watched in confusion as he walked to a lush bed of greenery that grew in the mossy rocks alongside the pool. Even as he broke a wildflower off at the stalk and returned, she didn't understand what he was doing.

"Pink larkspur," he said, tucking a blossom into the curly blond hair at her temple. "To free the wolf."

The pool seemed to come alive with anticipation as Edwina approached it a moment later. Staring down into its bubbling depths, she touched the waistband of her jeans. The feelings inside her matched the water's turbulence. She fingered the metal button on her jeans, and wondered if she could go through with it.

She had left Diablo back by the bike, standing in the shadows, but she could feel his eyes on her, and the thought that he was watching unnerved her so much, it made her hands shake. But it also excited her strangely, filling the pit of her stomach with a vibrancy unlike anything she'd felt before.

The sensations inside her were more sound than feeling—the sweet clamorous clutch and clang of bells. Vibrations sang along the fine network of nerves in her breasts. They honeycombed her belly and inner thighs. It was beautiful, and terrible, the sound. As she worked the button of her jeans loose and found the metal tab of the zipper, the bells sharpened, pealing out their excitement, until finally it was almost more than she could bear.

"Don't watch me," she said, her voice a whisper.

She hesitated, then rode the slide down with her fingers, sighing tautly as the teeth unmeshed. A sense of disbelief swept her as she watched the tiny teeth come apart. They separated as though in slow motion, torturously, one notch at a time. Her nerves jumped with each soft click.

Turn away, she told him silently. *Please—don't watch me.*

The jeans dropped to her ankles, and a delicate shudder took her as she stepped out of them and made a three-quarter turn. She couldn't bring herself to look at him, but she knew he was there, in her periphery.

Her skin was misted with dampness, and the clingy cotton top and panties she wore seemed part of her flesh. She crossed her arms and grasped the hem of the shirt in her fingers, drawing it up until her midriff was exposed, then hesitating as anxiety soared inside her.

"Turn away," she pleaded softly, looking up. It took her a moment to locate him in the dark. As she did, she realized two things that astonished her. The first struck her with nearly physical force. His back was to her! He hadn't been watching. She had asked him not to, but it never occurred to her that he would honor the request.

The second realization shocked her to the core. She *wanted* him to watch. "Diablo, I—"

She saw his head lift, and her breath caught. She waited, but he didn't turn, and his hesitation forced her to try and finish the sentence. "I want you to—"

"You want what?"

He began to turn, and Edwina thought she would die of heart failure in the time it took him to come around. "To look at me," she breathed.

Even in the darkness, she could see his eyes. They were luminous, like animal eyes caught fire. Beautiful eyes, she thought. Demon eyes. Whatever responses she'd felt before were magnified a thousand times as she resumed her painfully awkward striptease. She couldn't look at the man watching her, but she was aware of him in every cell of her body.

Her breasts shimmered with sensation as she pulled up the top. Cool air touched her damp skin, and the shock of it made her dizzy. She heard the waterfalls roaring softly behind her and felt the clay soil give beneath her bare curling toes.

A sweet pain flashed through her limbs, but the most riveting awareness was the aching pull of her nipples. Their sensitivity brought back a sense-memory of his hands on her body. Rough, thrilling hands. Her flesh strained as she remembered how possessively he'd kissed and handled her. She'd bridled at his arrogance, but her body had responded. She still ached from his touch.

She caught one last glimpse of him as she drew the shirt over her head. He'd moved into the light, his hair flaring around him like a stallion's mane. Edwina shuddered with excitement and apprehension as she bared herself to the moonlight and to him.

The cavern went breathlessly silent.

The man went still, frozen in motion.

Somehow Diablo checked the feral impulse that had drawn him out of the shadows. Animal instincts burned high in his blood as he watched her. Now he understood why a stag would fight to the death over a female in heat. He'd wanted women before, but never as he wanted this one. Rage, he thought, feeling the kick in his groin muscles. He was in a sweet rage of need.

She was slightly built, almost boyish. Her breasts were small and and yet voluptuously formed. Aureoles the color of light caramel crested the delicate swells of flesh. God, it made him hard just thinking about her breasts. He could still feel them nestling in his palms like heavy cream.

She was made to give pleasure to a man, he realized, his groin muscles tightening as he imagined all of the ways in graphic detail. She was made to drive a man wild *before* he got the pleasure. He'd never known a female who could confuse and arouse the way she did. His strongest drive was to claim ownership, to take her lithe, trembling body and make it his, the sooner the better.

The low throb he felt intensified as he locked it away from his awareness. Unfortunately, it wasn't that simple. There was another drive, a conflicting impulse that he couldn't quite smother. He also wanted to protect her, improbable as that seemed at the moment. From predatory beasts like himself!

"You have a beautiful body, Princess," he said, his voice echoing harshly in the cave. "Show it to me."

She was naked except for the silk panties she wore—and the T-shirt that dangled from her fingertips as though she were afraid to drop it. Maybe it was the conflict in her that intrigued him. She was staring at him as though what he'd just asked of her was impossible, and yet he knew she was obsessed with the idea of making love with him, and had been since the afternoon they'd first met.

That knowledge hadn't come from any need to gratify his own ego. Some men could sense a woman's sexual threshold. There were plenty of giveaways—a scent, a nervous smile, a tension. Her quota was swollen, full to overflowing. He'd seen it in the dreamy cast of her mouth, in the way she touched herself. There was a voluptuary in Edwina Moody, a sensuous woman.

She toyed nervously with the lace on her panties

and then began to draw them down. It surprised him that she had a tan line, and at the first glimpse of untouched pink-and-white flesh, he felt a groan rise inside him. All of the turbulence in the cosmos seemed to be concentrated at the base of his body. Muscles stretched and strained and fisted.

As the panties dropped around her feet, she looked up at him, a question in her limpid amber eyes. *Now? Are you going to take me now?* her eyes asked.

Diablo felt as though all hell had burst loose inside him. The rules were clear, however. He had made them. He couldn't touch her until she took the flower out of her hair.

Edwina stood naked and trembling in the moonlight, her body continually misted by the fine spray from the falls. She was aroused and sweetly confused. She kept expecting him to come to her, and yet he didn't move.

"The pool," she heard him say.

The water was deliciously warm as she entered. Bubbles surrounded her with effervescence, and another sensation, luxurious softness. The minerals that fed the hot springs gave the water a satin texture, as though an exotic bath oil had been added. She made her way to the middle of the pool, immersing herself to her breasts. Little jets of foam surged against her limbs and her other parts. The sensations were indescribable, both stimulating and relaxing.

She looked up at Diablo, and even from a distance she recognized the fever in his eyes. He was waiting for her to release him, to release the wolf. Her heart accelerated as she reached up and touched the flower in her hair, and for the first time in their relationship she knew the subtle thrill of power.

Eight

Edwina took the flower from her hair and held it in her palm, examining its delicate pink petals. "Lovely," she murmured.

"Do you remember what it means?"

"Freedom?" She brought the blossom to her lips, drinking in its exquisite softness. The breath she released shook oddly. He was offering her something she desperately wanted—a taste of freedom, a chance to be something more than the dutiful daughter, the watchful big sister. He was offering her Edwina Moody, a woman she didn't know.

"Life has a flow, Princess. Give in to it."

Edwina had planned every step of her life for as long as she could remember, and so little of it had worked out the way she'd intended. Maybe it was time to take what came. Her shoulders rose with a sharp influx of air. Let go of the flower? *Let go of everything she knew?*

She set the larkspur blossom afloat.

The low sound Diablo made was rusty with heat and relief and sensuality. Edwina glanced up as he pulled off his boots and tossed them aside. He straightened, and her first impression was of dark eyes and flashing tension, a stalking wolf. Her next was of size, physical dimension. Perhaps it was her lower vantage point from the pool, but he looked enormous, a shadow thrown by the mountains.

His seeming disregard at shedding his clothes made the act even more startling as he stripped off the vest. With a quick flick of his fingers he popped the snap on his jeans.

Conflict rose in Edwina like a tidal surge, but she couldn't turn away. He lowered the zipper, and she could see by the V of dark hair in the widening slash that he wore no underwear. As he hooked his thumbs in the waistband to pull the jeans off, she stepped back and lost her footing. Water erupted around her, bubbles foaming and bursting. The pool went crazy with turbulence.

"Come on, Ed," he said softly. "You're not going to chicken out on me now?"

She looked up as she heard him pull off the jeans, and what she saw was enough to make her wonder about the old adage about all men being created equal. She'd seen him before, but he wasn't aroused then. He was now. Very.

She winced as he kicked the pants away. But she couldn't avoid his nakedness, or his arousal as he entered the pool. The warm water enveloped him, and when he brushed her cheek with his hand, she turned to him helplessly.

He stroked her face, a rare and sweet tenderness in his touch, and the strangest thing happened to her heart. It tightened and expanded. She could actually feel it squeeze and then swell in her chest as though to accommodate the surge of emotion she felt.

"You're *gentle*," she said.

"What did you expect"—a smile touched his eyes—"a wolf? The big bad wolf?"

"Yes." She had. Just that.

"Sorry." He pleasured her with lengthening strokes. "This may be a little boring then."

"I . . . doubt it."

Edwina dwelt for a moment in the crushing green of his eyes and knew that he *was* part wolf. His feral instincts might be in check at the moment, but they lived in the dark heart of him, waiting to be freed.

"What is your request?" she asked.

He looked surprised, and then he smiled. "Want to get it over with that quickly, do you?"

"No, I just want to know what I'm—what we're going to be doing."

"Rest easy, Princess, it's not that cold-blooded. I'll tell you when it's time."

"When it's time? But you looked so ready."

"Oh, I'm ready. I don't think I've ever been more ready. But this is an initiation, a solemn ceremony, and some things can't be hurried."

All the while he talked, he caressed her as though she were a purring kitten, stroking the underside of her chin as she tipped it up. *Mmmmmm*—on the tenth stroke or so, she decided that she could get to like him this way, tender and considerate.

"On second thought, there is something I want," he said. He held her with his eyes, running his hand up the length of her arm, riveting her as he cupped her breast. "I want this, Princess. And I want to watch your breath catch and your cheeks turn to flame when I take it."

Edwina obliged him. Her breath stalled high in her chest, and her nerve endings jangled like discordant bells.

He drew back to look at her, his eyes darkening as he continued to massage her breast. The warmth of his palm spread through her, feeding her nerves little shocks of desire. It was too much. Too exciting, too stimulating, *too close to pain*. Did he know that her nerves and muscles were tightening rhythmically with the pressure of his hand? Did he know he was eliciting stirrings and cravings the likes of which she'd never experienced?

His eyes said he knew everything, every little twitch of desire she felt. His eyes said he was only beginning.

She made a soft sound, nearer a moan than a sigh.

His breathing thickened.

"I need to kiss you, Princess," he said. "I need to do a lot of things to you."

Edwina's stomach dipped as he scooped her up and drew her closer, hooking an arm around her hips. "Are you allowed multiple requests?" she asked. "Is that in the rules?"

"I'm allowed whatever you'll give me."

He framed her face almost hungrily, letting his hand follow its contours. As he bent to kiss her, his fingers contracted, and his thumb sank into the flesh of her cheek. "Delicious," he said, tasting her lips. "You taste of the spring."

His body was making itself known to Edwina in startling ways. He was sinew and bone and hot, protruding parts. Everything she'd seen was now firmly thrust against her, pressing into her just as she'd fantasized. Male equipment. *Superb* male equipment. Her imagination went wild thinking about what he was going to do with all of it.

The parts he seemed most concerned with at the moment were his lips, and hers. "Kiss me back," he said, cupping her head and moving his mouth over hers with extraordinary slowness. There was a depth of sensuality in the swaying, drifting friction that Edwina couldn't resist. It was like being teased and tortured with silk chiffon. The oddest, sweetest yearnings were rising in her, and he seemed to be drawing them up with every drift of his mouth.

She murmured her pleasure and pressed into him, seeking deeper contact. Where there had been trepidation now there was a gentle welling of hunger in her. She was a woman aroused. A woman in physical need . . .

He locked her tighter to his body and made a low mesmerizing male sound.

This was all new ground for Edwina. She'd never had a man respond to her as he did. Something shivered in the pit of her stomach. A deep reverberating thrill. The sensation was beautiful and seductive, gathering energy to it like a magnet, draining off strength from other parts of her body. A languorous weakness seeped slowly into her limbs, part welling heat and part physical intoxication. She was high on charmed water. She was drunk on his kisses, dizzy with the taste of him.

Diablo felt a sigh quiver through her lips. She squirmed against him, slick and warm, all legs and arms and naked breasts. The woman was driving him *wild*, and suddenly he knew why. It wasn't just her pliant body. It was her impetuousness. She had the sexual inhibitions of ten women, and yet the way she blundered through them was irresistible, rushing in where angels feared to tread, surrendering herself in ways that even a more adventurous woman wouldn't have.

She seemed enraptured with the discovery of her own body, and quite willing to try anything. The combination was explosive, Diablo realized.

He cupped her buttocks with his palms and brought her up against him, an aggressive move that sent a shock wave of desire vibrating through his body. He could feel her delicate muscles tautening under his fingers. She was soft and slick to the touch. All female curves and firm flesh, unbelievably responsive.

"Gracious," she breathed, breaking away from him. Her eyes searched him, a little wild. "Please— tell me what it is you want," she implored. "I'll do it, whatever it is, I promise. Lord, I think I *want* to do it."

He sank his fingers deeper into her springy flesh and thrust himself against the satin cushion of her belly. "This is what I want," he said, his jaw clenching. Another laser of desire shot through him, bombarding that hot spot at the base of his body.

"I want to tamper with every inch of you in one sweet, sexy way or another." His eyes darkened, and his voice went soft and husky as he brushed his lips near her ear and whispered, "And then I want to get into you, Princess . . ."

She whimpered plaintively as he began to thrust

rhythmically against her. "Deep and tender," he said. "Just like this. All of me. Into all of you."

Edwina nearly dissolved in his arms. She felt as fluid and bubbly as the water swirling around her. She couldn't stop the sounds that stirred in her throat or the fizzy magic in her stomach. He ran his hands up her body to her breasts, cupping them roughly, tenderly, and she melted into him—fragile, submissive, utterly languorous.

It was all Diablo could do not to take her right there in the pool. His mind was torturing him with images of her vibrant body rocking against him, shuddering under his deep thrusts. He could almost hear her crying out in pleasure. His mark was on her body, a symbol of his possession. It was time to stake his claim in a purely physical way. And yet something was blocking him.

He tipped her head back, searching her eyes. She looked so damned vulnerable, the thought of hurting her made him ache. Did she really know what she was doing? Or was he again taking advantage of some deep deprivation she couldn't control? "What am I going to do with you, Princess? Save you from yourself? Or ruin you?"

It took her a moment to register the question, but once she had, she didn't seem to have the slightest concern about his noble conflict. "Oh . . . I definitely think you should ruin me. In the meantime, can I touch *you*?" she asked. "Is that in the rules?"

Diablo exhaled heavily. "To hell with the rules."

She glided her palm down the muscles of his back, drifting over his buttocks with a quick caress. Energy surged in his groin, and the impact was more pain than pleasure. He'd been aroused since even before she'd stripped. Now he was agonized. The hell with protecting her, he thought as her curious hand crept nearer and nearer to that wildly sensitive part of his body. His stomach muscles knotted.

She touched him where he hurt most, and he couldn't suppress a groan. "What are you doing?" he said. "This is supposed to be *your* initiation."

"Oh, my," she said, sobering a little as she traced a finger up the length of him. "You really are . . . ready."

"Edwina, you're making this—"

"Hard?" Her eyes twinkled.

"Difficult." He breathed a short harsh word as she touched her fingertips around him, slipping them down the length of him like a delicate sheath. It was ludicrous to say he wanted her, an understatement of massive proportions. *He had to have her.* It wasn't just physical anymore. It was body, mind—maybe even his eternal soul if he had one. Every fragment of his being demanded it.

"Turn, Princess," he whispered. "Turn and open your legs for me."

"What?" She couldn't. Even the idea shocked her. All of Edwina's dreamy, languid yearnings went silent as she realized what he intended to do.

His eyes flashed a transfixing emerald green, and he turned up the heat a little, kissing her slowly, dipping his tongue into the sheath of her parted lips. "Turn, baby, do it for me. It's time."

Time, Edwina thought. He was invoking the bargain they'd made. She had freed the flower, and with it her right to refuse him anything. She stared up at him, only to breathe out a soft shocked word as he reclaimed her breast. The wonder of his touch sent a spear of delight straight through her.

Lord, how could she refuse him anything? She went soft inside when he touched her. She felt plucked at, like the strings of a mellow guitar. His finger strokes vibrated through her, thrumming softly at her nerves. She might have resisted quick hot passion but not this sweet, insistent battering. Not this slow, overpowering seduction of her nerves and senses.

He bent and took her lips, and Edwina could almost hear the poignant strains of music stirring inside her, the low lush riff of a tenor sax, the upswing of a moody clarinet. It was a deep bluesy sound, rich and melancholy in its resonance. She closed her eyes, reveling in it, letting him kiss and nip softly at her lips. And then she heard the wondrously husky voice of her music maker.

"Turn, Edwina."

She responded to her own name automatically, her body flowing with the gentle demand of his hands. When her back was to him, he pulled her flush up against him, his hands moving over her as slowly and sensually as the water. His arousal pressed into the tender swell of her buttocks, and it could easily have been the most thrilling sensation Edwina had ever felt in her life.

"Ah, Princess," he said, cupping her breasts, "you couldn't possibly know how good you feel this way." He flattened his palm to her belly, massaging gently as he pinned her up against him. Each rhythmic thrust of his hips sent a shudder of delight through Edwina.

She knew exactly how good *he* felt. She was aware of several things at once, all of them breathtakingly erotic. His hands were lightning rods to her nerves, drawing sparks everywhere he touched her. His body was a miracle of masculinity—aggressive, invasive, all thrusting energy. He was hot and muscled against her back. Hot and muscled all the way down to her toes.

A sweet aching need arose in the deepest part of her. Her body was creating its own miracle. Her body wanted what he had, all that heat and muscle, all that superb male equipment. She tightened at the mere thought of it, and the next thrust of his hips set her off like a lighted firecracker. She was taut. She was weak. She hardly knew what to do next. Sighing helplessly, she let her head fall back as he nuzzled her neck.

"That's it," he murmured, his breath warm against her ear. "Stay with me, baby. Stay with me."

Edwina was dreamily aware of the circular motion of his hand as he pleasured her. Seconds later, she drew in a sharp breath as he began to give equal time to the back of her anatomy. Her eyes came open as his fingers trailed over her hips and finally her buttocks, arousing the nerve-rich area. She stiffened, astonished at the lightning reactions.

A sudden urgency flared in Edwina. She couldn't hold still under the drift of his fingers. His touch was drenchingly erotic on her skin. A soft insistent throb swelled inside her, and she began to move in response to its steady pressure. It seeped into her consciousness, that hot sweet throb, saturating her.

His breath was hot against her ear. "Open your legs for me, Princess."

She felt his knee press against the inside of her thigh and responded without thinking. Warm silky water rushed through her legs as she opened them, and suddenly his hand was there, caressing her thigh where his knee had been. She stifled a gasp of pleasure. He knew just how to touch her, just *where* to touch her! His strokes were slow and murmurous, drawing up sensations she could hardly bear, they were so sharp.

Edwina felt deep muscles pull tight inside her.

"Easy, Princess," he said, gentling the nape of her neck with kisses. He continued to run his fingers along the back of her legs, sprinkling sensations along her inner thighs. And then he eased her body forward slightly and began to touch her in ways she'd never been touched.

He locked an arm around her waist, holding her gently, but even if he hadn't held her, she would have been helpless against such forbidden stimulation. "It's all right," he said as she let out a shocked sound. "This is all I want for now, Princess. Just to touch you."

His hands brought her the most riveting kind of pleasure she'd ever known and something much more urgent. Her body went soft and wet and languid under his caressing, probing fingers. Desire. She was melting in a spring flood of desire.

"You're made just like the flower, Princess," he said. "Soft and pink and sweet."

He explored the satin folds and petals until she

was weak with need. And then he delved deeper. Edwina gasped as he began to probe, long fingers caressing her inside and out. Deep muscles clenched urgently, and her tender parts throbbed with pleasure. Unable to stop herself, she began to answer the slow beat of his strokes with a writhing motion.

Diablo knew a violent wrench of excitement as she moved against him. He'd never experienced a woman more female, more urgently sensual. He could almost take his pleasure in just giving to her. Almost. His body ached with the need to know a woman's secrets again. He'd denied himself for far too long, and the heat of sexual conquest was in his blood.

She breathed an agonized sound as he tried to withdraw. "No!" she cried, her muscles fluttering and tightening around him. His jaw muscles clenched as he left the silken vault and pulled her up against him.

"It's okay, Princess," he said, tilting her head back for a kiss. She tasted of springwater and desire. It was crazy, but at the moment she tasted like everything he'd ever wanted in life. "I've got a better idea," he said.

"Me too." She pressed her lips to his. "Make love to me. Make love to me until I can't breathe."

He tried to draw her around to face him, but she resisted. "No, like this," she said.

Diablo was rocked by surprise. She wanted it this way? From behind? Everything that had been sensual and slow before suddenly became immediate and urgent. There could be no more delaying, no more holding back. *He had to have her.*

"Yes . . ." She breathed out the word as he pressed her upper body forward and caught her by the hips to steady her. He found her silky heat almost immediately, as though some instinctive primal force were guiding him. The urgency between his legs became a hard throb as he probed her gently, readying her until the pain and pressure of his own body drove him wild.

A fierce sound welled in his throat as he braced

her with his hands and eased into the heat of her. She gasped softly, and for one blissful second they were on their way to heaven. And then he met the sweetest, tightest resistance he'd ever known in a woman.

"Easy, baby," he said, caressing her hips and thighs with his hands. She was built small, but he'd had no reason to think she couldn't accommodate him. He knew she wanted him. He thrust again, and she let out a soft excited sound.

"Relax, Princess," he said, grasping her by the waist. But even as he repositioned her, he knew it wasn't going to work. She *couldn't* relax. She was frantic. He pressed into her again, but the thrusting only aroused her more, and she gave out a sharp cry of frustration.

"I'm sorry, Princess," he said, releasing her. He pulled her into his arms and shushed her with kisses and tender words. "Give me a chance, baby. We'll make it right."

A moment later he had her wrapped in a blanket from the saddlebags. The grotto was studded with soft beds of ferns, and he settled her on the nearest one.

"Let's start this all over," he said.

Edwina gazed into his eyes and saw a tenderness there she'd never seen before. He looked so ruggedly handsome that something gave way inside her. Heat stung her eyelids, and she blinked away moisture that might have been tears. No, she wasn't crying. She just wanted him so badly, she thought she was going to die, that was all.

Diablo saw the flicker of hurt in her eyes, and it stabbed at him. "What is it, Princess?"

She shook her head. "Nothing. I just want you to make love to me!" She touched her fingers to his parted lips, and her voice trembled. "Would you do that, please?"

In that one naked moment, Diablo felt an emotion that he barely understood. He didn't know its name, but it was squeezing his heart. Suddenly he was racked with tender feelings, confusing feelings. He wanted her so badly, it was like a knife turning in his gut, but he couldn't hurt her. God, he wasn't sure he could handle it if she cried.

Edwina saw his hesitation and grew quiet. His sensitivity was a wondrous thing to her, totally unexpected. A moment later she drew off the blanket that covered her body and gazed up at him in lush, silent invitation.

Diablo took in the creamy nakedness that had driven him crazy just moments before and felt a wrench of need in his groin. Lord help him, she was beautiful. Somehow the whisper of sadness in her eyes made her even more mesmerizing as she lay there before him, suppliant, waiting, her breasts glowing in the moonlight.

He moved over her and sampled her lips, a hunger rising in him. She arched and moaned, presenting him with such perfect breasts, he had to taste them too. He suckled her sweetly, assuaging one kind of hunger and feeding another. The hardness he pressed into her belly was an aching thing that he knew only one way to satisfy.

Edwina melted under his tender assault. She was beyond needing him. She yearned. She was delirious. And when at last he spread her legs and pressed himself against that tender, aching part of her, she breathed his name like a prayer.

His lips touched hers, and he entered her body slowly. So slowly. It was beautiful, nerve-racking pressure, throbbing love one inch at a time, and Edwina had never been so exquisitely possessed. The restraint showed in his features, making them more gaunt, more beautiful. The holding back was torture, and yet he continued his maddening pace, pressing into her, loving her a little at a time, waiting until her body yielded and took him completely.

But Edwina was impatient. She was urgent. She needed him there, fully there, and by the time he was, she was already in the throes of some glorious, torturous convulsion.

Diablo felt her peaking. He scooped her up and

held her tightly, letting her cry and shatter around him. It robbed what was left of his will not to finish with her, but he needed more time in the grip of her beautiful body. He had held back so long that nothing could satisfy him now but a savage shuddering physical release. It wasn't a choice anymore. It was a reflex as fundamental as breathing. He had to have her, he had to take her again and again, thrusting, thrusting until he was spent, not stopping until at last he had stamped out the fires raging in him.

As he laid her back down and gazed at her flushed face, he felt the power of what they were doing. And the risk. Something in her total acquiescence made him want to cover her face with kisses and whisper tender things to her. There was wonderment in her eyes, rapture in her sigh.

"I have to take you again, Princess—my way. I have to take you fast and hard and deep, or I'm going to die."

She arched up and caught him as he drove into her. A cry ripped free, plaintive and primitive. In the vibrant collision of their bodies, Diablo had no idea who had made the sound. All he knew was a pure raging joy as he unleashed the wildness in him.

He rocked and thrust and drove into her with unbridled passion, fighting the inevitable as her sharp shuddering cries pushed him closer and closer to the brink. When at last he tumbled off, it was with a sense of falling uncontrollably, of cartwheeling through space. He was a blindfolded man who had stepped off the edge of the world.

Nine

"Is that the Big Dipper?" Edwina asked. She rested her head on the arm Diablo had curved around her shoulders and looked up at the starry firmament. They were sitting up now, wrapped in the blanket for warmth, and Edwina was in an especially dreamy mood. She pointed toward a generous wedge of night sky ablaze with starfire.

Diablo followed the line of her finger and shook his head. "No . . . that's not the Big Dipper, but it looks a little like it. That's Draco, the dragon star."

She swung around to look at him. "You know astronomy?"

"I know the dragon star," he said. "The Warlords consider it their lodestar."

"Oh . . ." She fell back against his arm, but her heart felt light, and her senses were alert. Chris Holt was an astronomy buff, and for a moment she'd thought—

She glanced again at Diablo's features, remembering how nonchalantly he'd handled the snake. She'd assumed that with his Spanish nickname and long dark hair he had some Mexican or perhaps Indian blood. And yet those green eyes.

"A lodestar?" she questioned, studying his profile. "Isn't that a bit philosophical for the Warlords?"

"The brothers are more evolved than you think," he said, laughing, kissing her nose.

Edwina made a face and suppressed the answering smile that welled in her heart. It was hard to stay focused on anything serious when she was nestled next to a naked man in a blanket. Especially *this* man. He was warm and alive. He was certifiably real in a world that seemed like a misty soft-focused dream. All around them the cicadas sang their hearts out, and the waterfalls babbled like excited children. Edwina identified totally with the sweet riot of noise. She felt like an adolescent who'd been knocked for a loop by her first crush.

"Do we have to go back?" she said. "It's so beautiful here."

"We don't have to do anything, Princess."

He hugged her close, and there was such a wealth of husky conviction in his voice that Edwina's throat tightened. He sounded as though he meant it, and in her heart she wanted to believe he did. Maybe it was crazy. Maybe it was moonlight and rarefied mountain air, but hidden away from the world as they were, she felt as though they could be the only two people on the planet. The last man and woman. Adam and Eve in some new incarnation.

Oh, Edwina, she thought, *now you have lost your alleged mind.* She wanted to dismiss the idea, quickly, summarily, but that didn't seem possible. Some untamed part of her heart wouldn't let it go. The last man and woman. Making love, making babies, living off the land. She released a little sigh as she thought about how perfect it would be. . . .

And how perfectly ridiculous. A fantasy, she told herself. She was a woman amusing herself with idle dreams and romantic whimsy. Too much time on the back of a motorcycle, undoubtedly. But even pitted against cold logic, the impulse wouldn't be denied. She didn't want to go back to camp or to the rodeo, or even to Connecticut. She wanted to stay right here, with him. Of course it was crazy. It was impossible. She had obligations, people depending on her, and yet she actually felt as though she wanted to be with him to the exclusion of everything and everyone else. It was like a fire burning deep in her heart, waiting to be fanned, pleading to be fanned. There was a word for what she was feeling, she realized, a dangerous word. *Longing.*

"Are you shivering?" he asked, drawing the blanket around her.

She shook her head, but she was, of course. After a moment she drew the blanket off her shoulder and began to trace the tattoo, engrossed in its tongues of fire. "I guess it's official, huh?"

He watched her for a while. "Yeah . . . you're mine."

Edwina's jaw muscles ached from her attempt not to smile. The fire burned a little higher in her heart as she dwelt in his eyes for one unguarded moment. "Maybe we ought to try it again soon," she said. "The initiation, I mean. Just to make sure it took."

He laughed softly. "Whenever you want, Princess."

She blushed a little. "We didn't actually finish what we started in the pool."

"I think that has something to do with the way you're built."

Her answer came with a flashing grin. "Maybe it's the way *you're* built."

He kissed her again, lightly, touching the bridge of her nose and working his way down to her lips. Long fingers combed into her hair, and things were just getting interesting when his mouth strayed from hers. "You do know that tomorrow's the last day of the rodeo?"

Edwina nodded, terribly disappointed that he'd reminded her. But she also detected another response in her own quick expiration. Perhaps it was relief that he was bringing them both back to reality. Her fantasy world was getting dangerous.

"And you do have a man to track down, don't you?" he added.

She looked up at him, surprised. "I thought you didn't want me to talk about that?"

His shrug said things were different now. And he

was also curious, she realized. There was an alertness behind his casual posture.

"What do you want with this Holt, anyway?" he asked.

"It's personal, a family thing," she said evasively, "*his* family." It wasn't that Edwina didn't trust him. She'd been trained not to reveal any more information than was absolutely necessary. As soon as people knew you were looking for the missing heir to a fortune, long-lost relatives popped up everywhere.

"How's the search going?"

"I'm narrowing things down." Again, Edwina wondered just how much she should tell him. He might be able to help her, and since tomorrow was the last day of the rodeo, her time was running out. "What do you know about Killer?" she asked.

Another shrug. "He plays the stock market."

"Exactly. And it so happens that the man I'm looking for comes from a family of stockbrokers —Braxton Securities. Benjamin Braxton, the fourth, is Holt's uncle." She watched for his reaction.

"So . . . you think Killer is Holt?"

"I think he could be, and I intend to find out."

He scooped a twig up off the ground and began to break it into smaller pieces. "Where's this Holt from?"

"East Coast, Connecticut area."

Diablo shook his head. "Killer's a native Californian. His dad owns a movie studio and a couple of theme parks. Hell, he's got four or five names, and none of them is Holt. Louis B. Mayer Killebrew, or something like that. His dad named him after a movie mogul. Probably why he goes by Killer."

"You're sure?"

"He's not hiding it. Ask him."

Edwina honed in on that immediately. "You said you didn't want me asking questions and arousing suspicions."

"Killer's okay. He's harmless."

"Now he tells me." She shifted impatiently to look at him. She doubted that Diablo knew it, but he'd just blown a week's worth of detective work. "Okay, then, since you didn't want me asking questions before, maybe *you* can answer a few now."

He smiled, agreeable. "Like what?"

"Like do you happen to know any bikers who are also Harvard Business School dropouts?"

He drew back skeptically, and then an ironic glitter crept into his eyes. "Gotta be Mad Dog, right?"

"Mad Dog went to *Harvard?*"

"Sure, can't you tell? The Ivy-League apparel, the shrewd intellect?"

"Hey! Could I get a straight answer here?"

"I was only kidding, Princess. Mad Dog crawled out of a swamp—a primordial swamp."

"No, really. What do you know about him?"

"What do *I* know? He changes his story so often, nobody knows anything about him. He even got drunk one night and told a bunch of us that he was an astronaut."

"But you must know what part of the country he's from?"

"I don't even know what planet he's from."

Edwina might not have logged a lot of investigative miles in her short career, but she knew when she was being put off with quick answers. "I guess I'll have to find out for myself," she said, settling back to look up at the night sky. The dragon star blinked down at her. "Come to think of it, there are several things I'd like to know about Mad Dog, including why he doesn't have an old lady. I thought that was the rule—"

Diablo pulled her back around to face him.

"Mad Dog doesn't have an old lady because he's a brain-dead thug," he said, his voice steely. "Rumor has it the woman he had with him when he joined ran off screaming one night and was never heard from again. Mad Dog is *bad news*, Princess. And I don't want you anywhere near him, is that clear?"

Edwina nodded, but there was no way she could do what Diablo was asking. The curly reddish hair, the harmonica, even the Harvard-dropout reference. Perhaps they meant nothing, but she had the distinct feeling that Mad Dog was a link to Chris Holt—if not the man himself. She also had a sneaking hunch that Diablo knew more than he was telling her.

Edwina and Diablo arrived at the rodeo at mid-morning the next day. Several of the gang were there to greet them, including Carmen, Squire, and Food Chain, whom it seemed Carmen had officially adopted. She had the pig on a leash and was hand-feeding him a BLT sandwich, which Food Chain scarfed down without so much as a peep about the bacon.

Diablo was quickly recruited for that morning's barrel-racing event, but not before he and Edwina suffered through the requisite number of crude jokes about their night of passion.

"Did she overheat your engine, Diablo?" someone wanted to know. "Poor dude's still smoking!" another agreed. "He'll be easy to beat today!"

Edwina was immensely relieved when Diablo finally herded the hooting bunch off toward the stadium. She glanced at Carmen next to her and noticed the Mexican woman following Diablo's easy stride. "Is something wrong?" Edwina asked.

Carmen flushed slightly. "I'm just surprised that you survived the night with that man. I would be dead from the pleasure."

"I almost am," Edwina admitted, joining Carmen in her appreciation of Diablo's considerable male magnetism. As he disappeared from view, Edwina felt an echo of the longing she'd experienced the night before. The fires within were still smoldering, she realized. *What was she going to do about her feelings for him?*

It wasn't until later that morning, when she and Carmen were seated in the stands watching the men compete, that Edwina finally had her chance to check out the information Diablo had given her. She dropped some casual questions about Killer and learned from Carmen that he was exactly who Diablo claimed he was, a studio executive's son. Not

Chris Holt. Carmen's knowledge of Mad Dog wasn't nearly so conclusive, however.

"He's new to the area," she said. "Nobody knows too much about him except that he's very secretive. I think his past may have caught up with him, though. There was a man here yesterday, looking for him. Weird guy in a trench coat."

"A black trench coat?"

"Yeah, that was him. He wouldn't say what he wanted."

Edwina decided against mentioning that she'd seen Mad Dog with the very same man. She wanted to keep Carmen talking. "When did Mad Dog join the Warlords?"

Carmen absently stroked Food Chain's pink ears. "I don't know, maybe six months ago. I never wanted him in the gang," she admitted. "But Squire figured it would be better to have a guy like him with us than against us."

"He is pretty intimidating," Edwina agreed, keeping the tone conversational. "I wonder where he's from originally?"

Carmen merely smiled. "He told Squire he was from New York. Said he rode with the Hell's Angels back east. He's always bragging about something. I don't believe half of it."

She shook her head and turned her attention back to the rodeo. "A Hell's Angel who plays the harmonica?" she said disdainfully, still tickling the pig's ears.

New York, Edwina thought. At least it was the right coast. She hadn't turned up any reference to the Hell's Angels in her research, but that didn't mean Holt hadn't ridden with them at some point. The other possibility, as Carmen suggested, was that Mad Dog had made it up. And if he was lying, he appeared to be going to a great deal of trouble to conceal his past.

While Edwina mulled the possibilities, she joined Carmen in the task of fondling Food Chain. The creature snorted in ecstasy as she rubbed the bristly underside of his snout. Hog Heaven, she thought, gazing into his bloodshot eyes. She did love animals, but whoever designed the pig must have been having an off day. "You do have nice cheekbones," she assured him, chucking his chin.

Food Chain sighed, and Edwina went back to the task at hand—Mad Dog. The next logical move would be to ask him some questions—not a pleasant proposition, but necessary. She was putting together a battle plan when a roar went up in the stadium.

Edwina looked up to see Diablo and his bike flying through the air. She rose, gasping with the crowd. The bike boomeranged off the stadium's chain link fence, and Diablo hit the ground, rolling and tumbling.

"Is he all right?" someone shouted.

Edwina was nearly sick with fright. The violent image swam in her head as she fought her way through a sea of bodies to get to the aisle. She couldn't see the field in her rush to descend the bleacher steps, and by the time she'd reached the bottom, a swarm of onlookers had blocked her view completely.

"Let me through!" she pleaded, frustrated in her attempts to penetrate the suffocating crush of spectators. More bodies crowded in on her as she tried to shoulder her way out of the mob scene. "*Please*—let me through!"

Desperate, she climbed onto a row of bleacher seats and made her way toward the exit. "Diablo!" she cried as a gap in the crowd opened up. He was encircled by bikers on the field, but she could see him getting to his feet. Yes, it *was* he, she realized. He was supported by Squire, but he seemed to be moving, walking.

Tears of relief burned Edwina's eyes, and she clasped her shaking hands together. "Let me get through!" she pleaded. "I'm his old lady!" But her frantic attempts to push through the pack were ignored. No one seemed to hear her, and the solid wall of bodies wouldn't budge.

That was when she saw Mad Dog.

He was half hidden in the shadows of the stadium, talking to the trench-coated man. Edwina's
heart was pounding, and the only thing on her mind
was getting to Diablo. She might not have even noticed the two men if they hadn't been directly in her
line of sight, but something about their conversation struck her as clandestine. A frightening thought
hit her as she worked her way toward the exit. If
there was any chance that the trench-coated man
was another investigator—a free-lancer, looking for
Christopher Holt on his own—then Edwina might
be about to lose the case—and her fee. It happened
all the time with big estates. Whoever got to the
missing heir first could make her own deal.

A siren wailed in the distance. Edwina wrenched
her attention away from the huddling men and saw
Diablo being helped out of the arena. Torn, she
began to push through the crowd again, glancing
back repeatedly to see what Mad Dog was doing. Her
heart froze as she saw Mad Dog and the man leaving. The impulse to follow them was overpowering.
All of her investigative instincts were triggered. If
she didn't find out what was going on, she might
not get another opportunity.

She jerked around again as the ambulance roared
up. Her view of Diablo was blocked by the people
streaming onto the field, but from what she could
see, he was on the ground, propped up against someone's bike.

"Diablo!" she shouted, waving. He looked up and
saw her then, his green eyes flashing in the sunlight. "Are you all right?" she cried.

He gave her a thumbs-up as the paramedics piled
out of the ambulance and flung open the back doors,
obscuring Edwina's view completely. Dear God, she
thought, her heart twisting with concern, was he
badly hurt? He had looked all right, but there was
no way to know for sure. She needed to talk to him,
touch him, see for herself.

She glanced back just in time to see Mad Dog and
the man disappear from view. Edwina was nearly

sick with indecision, but she finally broke her paralysis and began to follow the two men. At least she had to determine where Mad Dog was going and what he was doing. Then she could return to Diablo.

She followed the men across the fairground to the parking lot, watching them from the cover of a concession booth as they got into a four-wheel drive with California plates. They peeled out in a cloud of dust, roared down the road a short distance, and pulled off onto a heavily wooded dirt road that Edwina knew was not a through street. She'd seen the sign several times.

The car disappeared from sight, and Edwina glanced back at the stadium briefly. A filmy layer of perspiration covered her forehead. If she followed Mad Dog, she would have to go on foot. It was a devastating choice. If Diablo was badly hurt, she would never forgive herself, but she had to go. There was so much at stake—her family and home.

She was breathing heavily by the time she reached the underbrush that bordered the back road the men had taken. Following the rutted trail a short distance, she spotted the four-wheel drive parked in a narrow clearing in the trees. She approached slowly, using the foliage as cover. A twig cracked beneath her foot, and it sounded like a gunshot in the silence. Edwina's pulse beat went crazy.

She was about twenty feet away, close enough to get a direct look into the front side window, when she realized there was no one in the car. A shaft of sunlight poured through the empty cab, giving it a surreal appearance. Edwina made her way noiselessly through the brush and opened the car door, quickly scanning its interior. The keys hung from the ignition, and the ashtray overflowed with cigarette butts, one still smoldering.

Edwina was about to reach for the glove compartment to check the car's registration when she heard someone come up behind her. She didn't have time to react. An arm locked around her neck, and she was jerked backward out of the cab, off her feet.

The voice that snarled in her ear was terrifyingly familiar. "What in the hell are you up to?" Mad Dog asked, locking an arm across her windpipe.

Edwina couldn't answer. She could barely breathe. He dragged her backward as she flailed and fought, digging at the burly arm that was cutting off her air. Her lungs burned as though she'd inhaled acid. Static swam in front of her eyes, a sickening scatter of black and white dots that pulsed and swirled. She could barely make out the man in the trench coat as he stepped in front of her.

"I suppose we could throw her off a cliff," he said, staring at her as though she were a curious specimen of wildlife they'd tossed a net over. "Make it look like she slipped on some loose rocks. An accident."

Edwina must have blacked out then. All she could remember was Mad Dog's viselike hold, locking off her wind. The static engulfed her, a million tiny drops of ink bursting like black raindrops. The last images in her head before she drowned in darkness were Diablo's being flung from his bike and the screaming urgency of the ambulance. . . .

When she came to, she'd been thrown into the back of the four-wheel drive, a tarpaulin tossed over her. Her head throbbed, and her stomach slid with queasiness. She glanced around warily and saw Mad Dog and the other man exchanging packages alongside the car. They hadn't bothered to tie her up, and the clock in the car's dash told her that only moments had passed since she'd blacked out.

There seemed to be only two possibilities of escape: Slip out of the side door unnoticed, or somehow make her way into the front seat and drive the car out of there. Either way, her movements would probably alert them.

She tried the car-door handle first, holding her breath as she drew it down with excruciating slowness. She heard a slight click, and her heart nearly stopped. The men's low conversation was the only discernible sound. Straining to hear what they were saying, she let several seconds pass before she returned to the handle. She began to depress it, inch by inch, stopping instantly as the click sounded again.

Silence flooded her. And then all hell broke loose.

The world seemed to explode around Edwina. She ducked down into the cover of the car, protecting her head as the barrage erupted—staccato bursts of noise and sharp pops of light that she could see, even through her sheltering arms. It sounded like machine-gun fire, hundreds of machine guns all rattling at once. A devil's tattoo.

In the midst of the bedlam, a flash of darkness moved past the car. A man's cry of pain brought her up, and she saw the man in the trench coat crumple against the hood of the car. Diablo swept into her field of vision next. He dragged the man up and lifted him off the ground with one fist, planting the other solidly in the man's stomach.

Pungent gray smoke rose in a mushroom cloud, and the racket continued, deafening. Edwina stayed in the car for cover, and it was only as she scrambled into the front seat that she saw Mad Dog. The biker looked momentarily paralyzed, as confused as Edwina was by all the craziness and chaotic noise. With a howl of startled rage he turned and made a run for it, sprinting down the road.

Edwina acted on instinct. She twisted the key in the ignition, hit the gas pedal, and was flung backward in the seat as the car lunged forward. Laying on the horn, she barreled down the road after the fleeing man. A cry locked in her throat as she roared up behind him and spiked the horn repeatedly. The shock sent him stumbling off the road and into a thicket of brambles. Edwina swerved off too, chasing him deeper into the undergrowth.

Pinned by the car's bumper, Mad Dog spat out threats. He was hopelessly tangled in thorny vines, but that didn't stop him from kicking and clawing at the car's hood. Edwina was terrified he would break loose any minute. She honked the horn frantically and screamed for help.

Sirens wailed behind her. The car door flew open, and Diablo pulled her out of the cab and into his arms.

"Thank God," she sobbed, clinging to him.

Within moments sheriff's deputies had swarmed the area and apprehended both Mad Dog and his accomplice.

"What's going on?" Edwina asked as Diablo led her out of the smoke and chaos. "Diablo, what's this all about?"

"Let me get you out of here first," he said. "You've been through some hell."

"No," she insisted. "Tell me what's going on."

"It's a drug bust, Princess. You flushed out the action I was going after. I knew someone in the Warlords was running drugs. I just didn't know who it was."

Edwina gaped at him. "You're a policeman?"

He settled her on a fallen log and sat down beside her. "No, I'm not the law. I'm an investigative reporter. I've been trying to put a story together on the Warlords for months now. I was tipped that their run to Mexico might be more than a pleasure trip, but I wasn't expecting the deal to be cut until we crossed the border."

Edwina was still trying to assimilate what he'd told her. "You're not a biker? You're an investigative reporter? For a newspaper?"

"A newspaper reporter who rides a bike."

"Then your name—it's not Diablo?"

"I've got a lot of names, Princess, and Diablo is one of them. An alias comes in handy on a dangerous assignment."

A string of rough language brought Edwina's head up. "And this really is a drug bust?" she said, watching Mad Dog verbally abuse the deputies who were trying to handcuff him. She was still dazed by the sudden violence, but at least a few things were beginning to make sense—Diablo's desire to infiltrate the gang, Mad Dog's furtiveness. "What about the other Warlords? Are they involved? Not Carmen or Squire, I hope."

He shook his head. "Mad Dog's a loner. It looks like he was planning to use the club's runs to Mexico for cover."

A cloud of gray smoke wafted toward them. Edwina ducked into Diablo's chest, covering her burning eyes and waving the smoke away with her hand.

"Didn't care much for my fireworks?" he said, knuckling a smudge of soot from her cheek. His touch was gentle, his voice faintly amused.

"Fireworks? As in the Fourth of July? Cherry bombs and roman candles?" Edwina pulled back to look at him. "Is that what all that racket was? I thought the Marines had landed."

"That was the idea. I needed a diversion until the law got here, and—"

"Excuse me, sir, we're going to need to ask the lady a few questions." A young deputy sheriff hovered over them.

"The lady's not in any shape to answer questions right now." Diablo rose, dwarfing the nervous young man. "I'll bring her down to the station later."

"No, it's all right," Edwina assured them both. "I'd like to get it over with."

Persuaded, Diablo surrendered Edwina to the deputy's questions and went off to call his newspaper. Edwina was still badly shaken, but she recounted the entire incident to the deputy and assured him she'd testify if it became necessary.

Once she'd given her statement, she found Diablo tightening the chain drive on his bike. The machine's scratches and dents brought his accident rushing back to her. "Are you okay?" she asked.

"Yeah, I'm tough," he said, a grin flickering. "Let's get you out of here."

Edwina clung to him as they flew down the mountain on his motorcycle, away from the rodeo, away from the Warlords. Perhaps she'd always had an inkling that he wasn't really a biker, at least not a hard-core gang member. But an investigator like herself? That possibility had never occurred to her. He looked too wild and untamed. Too much like his dangerous name.

A realization hit her as they streaked down the highway. He'd saved her life. She could have been lying dead at the bottom of a canyon instead of very much alive and riding into the wind with him on the motorcycle. She closed her eyes and pressed herself to the warm strength of his back. He felt powerful and rock-solid, a balm to her shaky nerves.

She couldn't remember the last time a man had made her feel protected. Adrenaline was still zinging around in her chest, and her nerves were as bruised and tangled as the brambles that had snared Mad Dog. But she felt safe with Diablo and totally surrendered to his care.

She had no idea where he was taking her, and crazy as it seemed, she didn't care. She was alive. She was with him. Nothing else mattered. Edwina Moody, rescuer of pigs and people, had just been rescued herself. And the experience was transforming. She wasn't yet certain how it had changed her, but she knew that it had.

The mountain rushed past her as she turned to look at it. Sunshine bounced off great jagged rocks and stubborn, scrubby wildflowers. It was all beautiful, even the dusty brown creosote, and she would miss it desperately when the time came to leave.

She squeezed Diablo tighter and felt a thrill of surprise as he released a handlebar long enough to bring her fingers to his lips. His mouth was warm and insistent against the pulsebeat in her fingertips. Yearnings sprang up in Edwina, so sudden and sharp, they frightened her. Was it supposed to be this way? she wondered. Was passion supposed to ignite like a roaring brushfire? One look, and she wanted him. One touch, and she *had* to have him.

He stopped at a light and turned to her. The moment his eyes caught hers, it was done. He knew. Everything she was thinking, everything she wanted.

She'd never known anyone who could read her desires the way he could.

"Let me take you somewhere, Princess," he said. "A motel."

"Yes."

They careened off in search of a place, and Edwina simply couldn't keep her hands off him. She slipped her fingers under his vest and reveled in the hard smooth glide of his torso. He was vibrant and alive under her touch. Muscles rippled like crosscurrents beneath his skin. The feel of him was more than thrilling. It was a sensual remembrance. She ran her fingers through the hair on his chest and heard a soft groan as his nipples tightened under her fingertips.

She was wild by the time they found a room.

He had her clothes off before they reached the bed.

The fever in his touch, the urgency in his lips, was ecstasy to Edwina. She wanted to be crushed in his arms, thrown onto the bed and made love to with a passion that was soul-shattering. His lips bruised her tender skin and filled her belly with fire. It was torment—beautiful torment. She'd never known such need, such naked longing for physical completion.

He entered her, and she let out the soft shocked cry of a surrendering female. There would be no slow, sensual seduction this time. No tender coaxing of feminine muscles. He thrust deeply and recklessly, and she took him fully. A moan shook in his throat as he buried himself inside her. Buried himself alive.

Edwina dug her fingers into his flexing muscles. With each succeeding thrust the thrill intensified until he was so deeply buried in her body, so indelibly burned in her psyche, that she felt impaled to her soul with a fiery light.

The hunger was overwhelming. Both of them were helpless in the face of it. Diablo's body drove him mercilessly. He couldn't stop. Not until he knew every pore of her skin. Not until he'd heard every sweet whimper in her soul.

He clutched her to him in the final throes of his climax and knew that he'd gone too far. His body could be sated by any woman, but his heart could not. His heart would never be content with anyone but her.

Afterward, as he held her and their breathing returned to some semblance of normalcy, he pressed his lips to her silky blond hair. She moaned a little and snuggled into him, seemingly oblivious of everything, even the words he whispered in her ear.

"Edwina, we have to talk."

Ten

"Now?" she murmured, nestling up to his kisses. "You want to talk now?" She laid her head in the hollow of his shoulder and traced the dark hair ribboning toward his groin. "Couldn't we just do this stuff instead?"

He laughed softly, caught her marauding hand, and locked it firmly under the warmth of his arm. "You've got a one-track mind, woman." His smile was gradually replaced by traces of seriousness. As he released her hand, he turned it over and studied her palm intently, trailing her life line with his finger. "Edwina, I need to talk to you about the man you're looking for—Holt."

"Yes."

His finger stopped tracing. "You found him."

"Mad Dog? You mean Chris Holt *is* Mad Dog?"

"No . . . it's me. I'm Chris Holt."

"You?" Edwina's facial muscles went slack with surprise. All the reasons he couldn't be Holt scrolled through her mind as she stared at him. Chris Holt played the harmonica, he was afraid of snakes, he didn't have vivid green eyes or long dark hair. In the next flurry of seconds, she realized what she'd done.

She had forgotten the cardinal rule of investigation: NEVER ASSUME. She'd taken it for granted that he *couldn't* be Holt because of his reaction to the snake and the discrepancies in his physical description. She'd also let herself become emotionally involved, and that had undoubtedly fouled her instincts.

"I guess Columbo doesn't have anything to worry about," she said. "I really am one lousy detective, aren't I?"

His voice registered surprise. "Is that what you are? A detective?"

Edwina didn't answer him. Her mind was filling up with too many questions of her own. "The green eyes?" she asked, already anticipating the answer. "Your DMV stats say hazel."

"I wrote 'hazel' on the form. Nobody bothered to check."

She nodded. Of course. It was that simple. Bureaucracies were so damned inefficient, she could probably have gotten away with it herself. "What about the snake in my bag? You're supposed to be afraid of them."

"You're a better detective than you think you are, Ed. That almost worked." He laughed abruptly. "Snakes scare the holy hell out of me. But big boys aren't supposed to scream, are they?"

"And of course you play the harmonica?"

"Play?" A flicker of sensuality emerged with his smile. "I won't even try to tell you what I can do to a harmonica, Ed. It's *adult* entertainment, know what I mean?"

Edwina wasn't amused. "Then where is the thing? And why don't you play it?"

"My harmonica? Mad Dog won it off me in a poker game."

"Oh, Lord, a poker game?" She scooped the sheet around her and sat up, Indian-style. "Okay, let's get this settled. You say you're a reporter, but your employment history, such as it is, lists you as a laborer in a sweatshop, a stevedore, and a meat-packer, among other things. You're not on a newspaper's payroll, and if you're free-lancing, why didn't I come across a Christopher Holt byline anywhere?"

"Probably because I use a pseudonym. Most of my assignments are pretty dangerous, and the jobs you mentioned were my cover for the story I was working on at the time." He adjusted the pillow behind his head and gave her a wry, appraising look. "I did one on the Mafia a couple of years ago. Did my employment history happen to list me as a numbers runner?"

"Somehow they missed that."

"You seem to know a lot about me, Ed. Are you going to tell me what's going on?"

"One more question." She stared point-blank into his eyes. "If you really are Chris Holt, why didn't you tell me?"

"That's easy. I couldn't take the chance that you'd blow my cover with the Warlords. It seemed safer having you with me, where I could keep an eye on you, than letting you run around loose, asking questions."

He smiled faintly. "Call it a form of damage control."

"Thanks, I needed that."

"Don't underestimate yourself, Ed. You flushed out Mad Dog and handed me one hell of a scoop. I'm even going to give you a plug in my article."

"Should be good for business."

He swung off the bed, grabbed his jeans, and slipped into them. "Now, what's the story?" he said, turning to her. "I figured you were some sort of emissary from my uncle, sent to bring the wayward offspring home. He's tried that before."

"This *is* about your uncle." Even as she said it, Edwina realized she had no idea how he might take the news of his uncle's death. From appearances, they hadn't had a close relationship, but that didn't mean there might not be some emotional knots to untangle. Estranged relatives were often the most strongly affected by the death of a family member.

"When's the last time you spoke with him?" she asked.

"The night I walked out, fifteen years ago. You could call it bad blood. Very bad."

"Maybe you ought to sit down," she suggested.

He remained standing, and by the expectant set of his jaw she knew there was nothing to do but tell him what had happened. "Your uncle had a heart condition, although you probably knew that. He hadn't been well for years. I believe it was the stress of his business—"

She hesitated, wary of the tension that had crept into Diablo's features. "You didn't know he was ill?" she said, sitting forward, talking faster in her concern. "Oh, I'm sorry, I really am. There was nothing anyone could do. It was a coronary, but you should know that he didn't suffer. He died instantly, in his office."

The information seemed to hit Diablo with almost physical force. His eyes narrowed to slits and the bones of his face jutted through his skin as he stared at her.

"Oh, Lord—" Edwina hardly knew how to respond. She slid off the bed and wrapped the sheet around her, but he held up an arm as though to keep her away.

Edwina's intuition told her to leave him alone, and this time she listened to it. As he turned to face the door, she quietly picked up her clothes from the floor and began to dress. He would need time to come to terms with the news, she told herself. Perhaps she ought to leave and give him some time alone or at least wait until he was ready to talk.

But even as she dressed, she couldn't shake the feeling that something irreparable had just happened, something that would affect them in ways she couldn't even imagine. The premonition crept into the room's atmosphere like a chill draft of air.

He stood facing the door for so long that she finally spoke up. "There's an estate," she told him. "You've inherited a stock-brokerage firm, money, property. That's why I'm here. I work for an agency that locates missing heirs."

He made a half turn and looked her over. "You like that kind of work? Hunting down people? Profiting from a man's death?"

His eyes were so cold, she felt a shock of alarm run through her. "It isn't like that," she explained. "I'm not profiting by your uncle's death. I'm carrying out his last wishes. He wanted you to inherit, and if I hadn't found you, everything would have escheated to the state. Would you have preferred that?"

"Yes, I would have. The state can have it. I don't want anything of his."

His voice was unnaturally flat, with a disquieting quality that Edwina might have caught under other circumstances. In this case, she was more than a little dumfounded by his answer. She needed money desperately to hold her family together. It seemed impossible to her that he'd just inherited a fortune and was throwing it away. "But he left everything to you, Diablo, everything he had! He obviously cared about you—"

"What do you know about my relationship with my uncle?"

It sounded almost like an accusation. "Very little," she admitted quickly.

"Then spare me the Pollyanna crap. My parents died when I was a kid, and my uncle got stuck with me. I rarely saw him except to endure his lectures on upholding the family name and doing what was expected of me—a Braxton 'scion.' He always seemed to forget that my name was Holt."

Edwina remembered from her research that Chris's mother was a Braxton, the uncle's only sister. His father, Wiley Holt, came from "outside the family social circle," according to a newspaper account of the wedding.

"I know you're upset," she said, approaching him, "but letting the state have everything? What would that accomplish? Surely you won't let a dispute—an *ancient* dispute with your uncle—stop you from claiming your rightful inheritance. Even if you don't want the money for yourself, you can dispose of it in some responsible way. Charities or whatever. Otherwise—"

He breathed an obscenity that made her flinch.

"I don't give a damn about 'otherwise.' Can you understand that, Ed?" His eyes hardened, frighteningly impenetrable as he turned to face her full-on. "I made sure of that when I walked out of his house fifteen years ago. His death doesn't change anything, not for me."

Edwina could hear the edgy inflection beneath his cold anger. On some level she knew it was pain fueling him, and she responded to it. His childhood must have been so much more difficult than she'd realized. She wanted to tell him that she understood how rough it could be, that she felt his inner struggle and sympathized, but she sensed the futility. If she offered consolation now, he would almost certainly deny the pain, and then he might even reject her.

She felt a wave of helplessness as his eyes flicked away, as though he had just dismissed the issue from his mind. There seemed only one safe way to reestablish contact at the moment, and that was by asking questions. "What happened?" she pressed, softening her voice.

"What do you mean?"

She wet her lips as his eyes returned to her. "Between you and your uncle. Something must have happened. It's in your voice—the hurt, the anger."

"You don't want to know what happened, Ed."

"Yes—I *do* want to know. Of course I do. I *care* about you." Even as she said it, she realized her feelings for him had gone well beyond the caring stage. Her feelings were staggering, but she couldn't deal with that now.

He turned away and jammed his hands in his back pockets, furious at something—at her, probably, for forcing the issue. She watched a darkness move through him, and the intensity of it frightened her. She had touched something explosive.

"Diablo—"

"My uncle did something I couldn't forgive him for," he said softly, savagely. "He told me the truth about my father."

"Your father? . . ." Edwina remembered coming across a series of old newspaper articles about Gillian Braxton's marriage to Wiley Holt over her family's violent objections. There'd been a tragic car accident a few years later, and both Gillian and Wiley had died. "What about your father?"

"He was a murdering bastard, according to my uncle."

"What do you mean? What did he do?"

A muscle in his jaw twitched violently, and Edwina was sure it was an echo of the pain he was denying. "I know it must hurt," she blurted. "Diablo, please—"

He brought himself under control then, erasing the sudden fury before her very eyes. His shoulders lifted and froze. His jaw set implacably. And what lingered in his eyes as he turned to her was icy and crystalline and frightening. She could almost imagine a molten anger that had hardened and cooled so swiftly that it had crystallized like the volcanic rock of the mountains they'd camped in. Whatever had happened in his past, she realized, he had buried it as deep as the tortured fissures in Carbon Canyon.

"I think maybe you'd better get out of here" was all he said.

Edwina stared at him, stunned. A desperation rose inside her as she realized that he meant it. He wanted her to leave. *He was throwing her out.*

"I can't leave," she told him, her voice grainy with disbelief. "Not until this is settled. I'll understand if you don't want to talk about your past, and I won't press you, I promise. But there's still the other thing— the inheritance." She was grasping at straws, anything to keep him talking.

"I settled that when I walked out fifteen years ago. It's done."

"No, it's not done." She implored him softly. "Your uncle owned a company. He had employees, men and women with families. What's going to happen to those people?"

He turned away from her. "That's not my problem."

Edwina went still then. For all her anguished sympathies, her responses were also tempered by the other concerns building inside her. Her own dreams had been shattered by the irresponsible actions of her father. The emotional devastation Donald Moody had left in his wake had convinced her that certain bonds had to be honored, no matter what. Family came first.

It was Diablo's attitude—or Chris Holt's—that she didn't understand. By his own admission, he honored no one but himself. No matter how badly his uncle might have hurt him in the past—no matter what his father might have done—Edwina believed there was a time when you had to set family feuds aside and handle your obligations. It was a conviction she felt strongly. It was a conviction she lived, but she didn't know how to express it to him.

"Will you go back, at least, to Connecticut?" she asked finally.

"No."

She caught back her rising frustration and her pride, and made it a personal request. "I live in Norwalk. You could fly back with me."

He didn't even bother to turn around. "Get off it, Edwina," he warned. "You did your job just fine. You found me, and now you can get the hell out of here. If you're worried about your fee, don't be. I'll see that you get paid whatever's coming to you."

The utter contempt in his voice stunned her. Did he really believe she was pressing him because of the money? After everything they'd been through together? "Oh, that's right," she said, deeply stung. "You asked me about my job, didn't you? You wanted to know if I enjoy profiting from dead men?"

He turned then, tossing back his hair like a restless animal. His blazing eyes told her to stop, to leave it alone, but she paid no attention. Her heart was too full of things that had to be said.

"No, I don't like what I do all that much," she told him, "but it earns me a living. I have responsibilities, but that's something you wouldn't understand.

What would you know about sacrifice, about putting your own life on hold to take care of other people?" Her eyes sparkled with tears. "I was going to be a gerontologist once. I was going to run a day-care facility for kids and senior citizens, Pollyanna as that may sound to someone like you."

His voice dropped to a harsh whisper. "Don't, Princess," he warned, raising his hand. A tremor seemed to shake his body. "Don't cry, dammit. And for God's sake, don't lecture me. You don't know anything about me."

She turned away from him, her mouth trembling. What had happened to them over the last few minutes? Where had the sweetness gone? She barely recognized the man in the room with her. He was cold and cruel. The harshness in his voice tore at her heart. No, she didn't know anything about him, not about this man. But she remembered the man who was passionate and fiery and tender. The man who saved her life and made love to her as no one else ever had. Or ever could. *Where was he?*

The tears welled again. Hot and stingingly sharp, they burned through all her attempts to hold them back. It hurt to reveal her own pain, even to admit that she was suffering in any way. She was so used to being the strong one, the caretaker. It was Edwina who'd held her baby sister and let her cry it out. It was Edwina who'd sat up nights with her distraught mother. Ed, the steady one. Eddie, the aspiring saint.

Her cheek muscles burned as she fought to control the emotion jolting her. She knew it was more than Diablo that had triggered the tumult inside her. It was everything he represented—adventure, freedom, life on one's own terms. She hadn't known she craved those things until now, until him. She hadn't known they could be so important. It had actually been wonderful to depend on someone else for a short time, someone as strong as he was, or seemed to be.

"What the hell are you waiting for?" he grated.

The tears spilled over as Edwina closed her eyes. Her throat tightened, refusing to let her speak or even swallow. Of course he was right. What the hell *was* she waiting for? There was no longer any reason for her to stay. Nothing more to be said, given how he felt. What woman in her right mind would allow herself to become involved with someone as selfish as he was, a man who felt no responsibility to anyone but himself?

The room was silent when she opened her eyes a moment later. All she could see at first was stained and peeling wallpaper. Even the floor tiles seemed to have yellowed and cracked beneath her feet. The tiny motel room that had blazed with their passion moments before was now cold and lonely, an ugly, alien place. She glanced down at the tight top and cropped jeans she wore and shuddered. She felt almost as naked as she had the first morning she'd put them on.

The incongruity of her situation crept into her awareness like a thief who'd stolen into the wrong house. How had Edwina Moody ended up in a small sordid room with a man she'd only known a few days? A man who sought out danger and wanted no ties to anyone. A man who had just proven he could be brutally cold and frightening.

"Go, Princess," he said. "Get out of here."

She looked up, her heart pounding. *Princess.* Why had he called her that now? It took her several heart-breaking seconds to realize that she was doing it again, grasping at straws. He wasn't even looking at her. He was staring off at nothing, waiting for her to leave, his face set in harsh brooding reflection.

But he *had* called her Princess, and she'd heard the break in his voice. Her feelings seemed to rip and tear at her like talons, promising heartbreak no matter what she did. The crazy side of her wanted to be with him, whatever the consequences. The rational side knew it was impossible. Even if he wanted her, which he quite obviously didn't. All at once she felt overwhelmed with the need to escape the bewildering situation, and him. To escape the claws that were ripping at her heart.

"Yes, maybe I should leave," she said with a jerky glance around the room to see if there was anything she'd forgotten. *Edwina, the efficient one,* she thought. Her voice sounded brittle and distant as she spoke. "No need to drive me anywhere. I'll call a cab from the office."

Diablo heard the door click shut behind her, and the sound of it slammed into him like a gunshot. By the time he'd turned to the room's one grimy window, she was going through the saddlebags on the motorcycle, sorting out her stuff. A moment later, clutching the few things she'd brought with her, she headed toward the office.

He despised what he'd just done to her, despised himself for hurting her, especially when she couldn't possibly have known what she was getting into. His breath condensed on the windowpane as he watched her stumble on a loose rock and wrench her ankle. She was fighting tears and was swearing like a trucker if the rapid movement of her lips was any indication.

A bittersweet smile touched Diablo's heart, and the impulse to go to her was as explosive as anything he'd ever felt.

He pressed a fist to the pane, pushing until his knuckles were bloodless. He would bring her only grief. Nothing else would come of it. Their passion wasn't enough. It never could be enough. They were from different planets. She didn't know it yet, but she was born to be the wife of some nice straight-arrow guy, a minister or a public accountant.

As she disappeared from his sight, a numbing certainty came over him. Edwina Moody was going to be fine. Just fine. She would wake up one day, blink her soft brown eyes, and her prince would be there. Happy ever after.

He rubbed the blood back into his throbbing knuckles. It was Chris Holt he ought to be worried about. What did the noble refugee from life need? A coldness swept through him as he turned away from the window. Exactly what he'd always needed. Another assignment, another trip into some dark anonymous hell. That was the sure way to forget everything but surviving to live another day. Beyond that, all he needed was a motorcycle, a fast road, and the wind in his face. Nothing else. No one else.

Not at all sure of her reception, Edwina paid a visit to the Warlords the next morning before she caught the plane for Connecticut. She couldn't leave without some explanation, and she wanted to say good-bye. Perhaps she was also hoping to see Diablo at the campsite. There was no sign of him, however. The clearing where they'd slept and ate and had a fish fight was uninhabited. The charred logs and campfire ashes were the only visible reminder of their time together.

She found Carmen and the other women packing up for the last leg of the run to Mexico. Edwina approached them tentatively, relieved when Carmen beckoned her over.

"Where's Squire?" Edwina asked, noticing that all the men were absent.

"Fishing," Carmen explained with a long-suffering smile. "They're *all* fishing."

Edwina managed an answering smile. "At least they're not hunting." She looked around. "Speaking of which, how's Food Chain?"

"Squire took him along. They're inseparable."

With a mischievous twinkle in her eye Carmen waved Edwina over to a classic Harley Davidson motorcycle that had been customized, chopped, and fitted out with a sidecar. "It's Killer's bike," she said. "Since he doesn't have an old lady at the moment, he has the honor of chauffeuring Food Chain around."

"I'll bet he loves that."

"I don't know about Killer, but the pig's a happy camper."

As the women's laughter subsided, Edwina remembered what she'd come there to do. Generously including Diablo in her apology, she explained to Carmen that sometimes people had to do the wrong thing for the right reason. "Diablo had a job to do," she said. "I didn't know what he was up to myself until Mad Dog had been apprehended." She touched Carmen's arm. "Anyway, neither of us meant you any harm."

Carmen smiled reassuringly. "Diablo's been here already," she said. "He and Squire talked. I think everything's okay."

He'd been there? Edwina wanted to ask a million questions. How had he looked? Had he mentioned her? Where had he gone? Instead she nodded and smiled, although it nearly destroyed her to pretend such nonchalance. "That's good," she said lamely, suspecting that Carmen was waiting for her reaction. "I'm glad they resolved it."

"I guess you and Diablo won't be riding to Mexico with us?" she asked.

Sadness shadowed Edwina's smile as she took one last look around the campground. It was hard to believe now that she'd actually ridden with the Warlords and shared their nomadic existence for several days. "No, we won't be going with you," she said, a catch in her voice as she added, "But you have a good time, hear? And take care of Food Chain for me."

"Champagne?" a male voice asked.

"What?" Edwina was jolted out of her reverie by a pair of smiling green eyes. Her heart nearly stopped before she realized it was simply the airline attendant doing his job. The cross-country flight had been overbooked, and she'd been bumped up into business class where drinks and snacks were complimentary.

The attendant held up the bottle, waiting for her answer.

"No, thanks," she told him. She barely had her head above water emotionally speaking, and a drink would take her to the bottom like an anchor, she had no doubt. The attendant moved on to the next passenger, and Edwina studied him for a moment. He was short, blond, and scrupulously neat. Nothing like Diablo. All it had taken to stop her heart was that fleeting glimpse of green.

A sigh welled. She supposed that now every other man she met would have green eyes. Why was it always that way when you hurt? she wondered. The most innocuous things took on the power to bring pain, and suddenly they were everywhere, reminders of what you'd lost, visual land mines placed along the path of the brokenhearted. It was almost as though the cosmos was having a little joke at the jilted lover's expense.

The irony in her smile was laced with heartache. Cupid must have been a mean little cuss, she thought, shooting arrows through people's hearts. She certainly felt as though she'd been hit with something surgically sharp, a dart that had pierced her without benefit of anesthesia. Sometimes the pain came at her so unexpectedly, so jaggedly, that she wanted to draw into herself like a wounded animal.

Where was he now? she wondered. What was she doing? She caught her lower lip between her teeth, wondering if she'd done the right thing by leaving. He'd been cruel, but people in pain *were* cruel. The brutal references to his father and his past still haunted her. Maybe if she'd swallowed her pride and refused to leave, he would have opened up to her.

She shook her head and felt the heat of tears beneath her eyelids. His near rage was seared in her memory like a scar. A poignancy flared through her heart as she realized that he would have thrown her out bodily if she'd tried to stay. He would have brutalized her, not physically perhaps but in every other way.

She shook off her own pain then, unable to deal with it and refusing to torture herself any longer. She was being utterly foolish, as usual, trying to repair something that was irreparably damaged. She couldn't have stayed in California, even if she'd had the courage. She had responsibilities.

When the pilot announced their landing at Kennedy an hour later, Edwina felt the full weight of those responsibilities pressing in on her. She hadn't called home once during the time she'd been gone. It wasn't deliberate—she'd simply been swept up by the things that were happening to her. But her mother would never understand that. Katherine Moody would be frantic. Especially since it was totally unlike Edwina not to check in. She called home several times a day when she was working out of the Norwalk office just ten miles away.

There was also the tax lien. She had used up more than a week of the grace period, and even though she'd found Diablo—or rather, Chris Holt—there was no guarantee that she would be entitled to her fee since he'd refused to claim his inheritance. Given his state of mind when they parted, she wasn't going to put much stock in his promise that she would be paid.

She sighed and let her head drop back as she imagined trying to calm her mother's fears. Both Katherine and Beth depended on her so heavily. Perhaps too heavily. They would have to be prepared for the worst, Edwina realized, but she also knew that the Moody women would survive, even if they lost their home. They could take an apartment. They wouldn't be out on the street, for heaven's sake.

Staring out the window as the plane descended, she reflected on her imminent homecoming. She touched her shoulder where the tattoo still lurked beneath her blouse, and a bemused smile surfaced as she remembered her other physical changes—freshly tanned skin and tousled, sun-bleached hair.

Edwina Jean, what's happened to you? she thought, imagining her mother's reaction.

A lot had happened to Edwina Jean. A sweet terrible lot. She wasn't entirely sure herself who this woman was that she was bringing home to Connecticut. Yes, there were going to be several shocks in store, she realized. For all the Moody women.

Eleven

"You've killed Mom, you know." Beth Moody stood flat-footed and slitty-eyed in Edwina's bedroom doorway, her arms crossed like a hanging judge about to hand down a sentence. "You've absolutely killed her."

Ignoring her sister's theatrics, Edwina continued unpacking her suitcase. She pulled out the white top she'd worn in California and without thinking brought it to her cheek, closing her eyes for a moment against its softness. It still felt warm with life. It smelled of campfire smoke and larkspur petals and passion. It smelled of him.

"*Edweeena!*" Beth plunked herself on Edwina's bed and resumed her glowering. "Are you listening?"

Of course I'm listening, Edwina thought. But her throat tightened with sadness as she clutched the shirt in her hands. Memories tugged at her poignantly, and the scent of him pulled at her senses, softening her breathing, weakening her heartbeat. Her body seemed to be responding as though from memory. And even though she knew it was only a trick of her mind, she could feel herself being drawn in, irresistibly snared by a lingering narcotic passion. *His* passion. He was in her blood. He was still there, like a drug.

"Ed? . . ." Beth sounded worried.

Edwina shuddered reflexively. She was regressing

again, and she couldn't let that happen. She was in Connecticut now. It was over with him. It *was*. With an angry, shaking sigh, she walked to the clothes hamper and stuffed the top inside. One good wash cycle, some biodegradable detergent, a shot of Clorox, and that lost week in southern California would be gone forever, she told herself. Smells, men, motorcycles—all of it.

"Life goes on," she said with conviction, turning to her sister. "Yes, I am listening, Beth. In fact I can hear Mom walking around her room right now. If I killed her, Beth, why is she walking around her room?"

"Oh, you know what I mean—emotionally. She thought you were dead or raped or something." Beth rolled to her side, propped her chin on her fist and gazed at Edwina, wide-eyed. "And then she saw you kissing that biker on TV. Who was he, Ed? A Hell's Angel? He looked like a Hell's Angel."

"He was a Warlord, Beth."

Beth squealed. "A *Warlord*? Yikes! How did he kiss, Ed? Did he bite or anything? *Eeeeyuuuuu!* Did you like faint?"

Edwina scooped the rest of the clothes from her bag, walked to the hamper, and shoved them all inside. This really was too much. The possibility that her mother had seen the biker rodeo had never occurred to Edwina, although it should have. Katherine spent the majority of her days in bed, watching TV. In this case her mother had been a horrified witness to her elder daughter roping pigs and kissing an outlaw biker as if there were no tomorrow. She'd taken it badly, very badly.

Edwina let the suitcase lid drop with a sharp satisfying bang. It wasn't nearly as jarring as the emotions churning inside her, but it would have to do. She was about to haul the case to the closet when she heard her mother's soft voice behind her.

"Edwina, perhaps we should talk?"

Edwina's throat tightened as she turned to see her pale, delicately built mother standing in her doorway. Somehow it always brought her sadness when she was confronted with her mother's frailty. With her huge brown eyes and hesitant smile, Katherine Moody had the look of a gentle soul who needed protection from the world. And Edwina was her champion, it seemed.

"Yes, let's talk," Edwina said, signaling Beth to leave the room.

Beth made her exit, and Katherine walked to the stool that fronted Edwina's vanity and seated herself carefully. Edwina watched her in silent reflection, wondering exactly when it was that everything had gone wrong in their lives.

Since her father had gone, she'd come to think of her mother as more child than parent in many ways. Katherine had been ill with one thing or another as long as Edwina could remember. Occasionally, Edwina had allowed herself to wonder if Katherine's illnesses had driven off Donald Moody. She felt guilty even for the thought, but at the same time she couldn't help but notice that her mother's "spells" came and went with a certain regularity. Edwina could almost predict them now. Such as this very moment, she thought. Katherine was definitely on the brink of a crisis.

"I don't mind so much that you didn't call," Katherine said gently. "But I was hurt that you didn't tell me about the man. Who is he, Eddie?"

"It doesn't matter, Mom," Edwina said, trying to forestall any more discussion on the painful subject. "I won't be seeing him again."

"But Eddie, all that long hair. He looked like a hoodlum—"

Edwina shook her head. "That was his cover."

"He's a policeman?"

"No, a reporter—an investigative reporter."

"It's just not like you, dear."

Truer words were never spoken, Edwina thought. It hadn't been like her at all. Perhaps that's why it had been so heartbreakingly wonderful. "Mom, we have some things to talk about . . . the bills, the house."

"No—not now, dear." Katherine's face went ashen, and she stopped the conversation with a raised hand. "I'm not up to that sort of thing at the moment."

Edwina could have predicted that response too. Her mother was forever finding ways to avoid discussing their financial problems, as though denying them meant they didn't exist.

"I may not be able to cover the taxes, Mom," Edwina persisted, gentling her voice. "If I can't, we'll have to move."

"Move?" Katherine looked horrified. "We've been here for over twenty years!"

Edwina went to her mother and knelt by the chair. "Then maybe it's time to move on. A change might do all of us good."

"What's come over you, Edwina? I won't be uprooted this way, driven from my home. You'll have to do something."

Edwina could feel her mother's panic, but she felt helpless to assuage it. Somehow Katherine had to come to grips with the reality of their situation. "I'm the only one working, Mom. Beth's in school, and you're not well. We have to live within our means."

Edwina reached for her mother's hand, but Katherine waved her away and pushed out of the chair. "I can't believe you're saying these things. You were born and raised in this house, Edwina." She broke off abruptly, fighting back tears, then turned and hurried toward the door.

Something gave away inside Edwina as she watched her mother's unsteady flight. "Mom, *please*—" she said. She caught back the floodtide of emotion inside her for a second before it all came surging out, things she'd wanted to say for so long.

"You've got to pull yourself together, Mom. You can't languish this way! Dad's gone. He's not coming back."

The sight of her mother's stricken expression was more than Edwina could deal with. She wrenched around and stared out her bedroom window at the sunstruck afternoon. "Life goes on," she said, her heart heavy.

There was no avoiding Katherine's trembling astonishment as she left the room. Edwina heard every choked sound. In the silence afterward she was sure she'd destroyed what little emotional resilience her mother had left. *There will be a crisis now*, she thought. *A terrible crisis.*

The ensuing days brought Edwina everything she'd predicted, and more. Katherine vanished into her room, refusing to speak to anyone, even Beth. The family doctor was summoned, and after a cursory checkup he pronounced Katherine physically sound but emotionally exhausted. Doom and gloom prevailed, with Beth mumbling incessantly about Edwina's "killing" their mother, and Edwina wishing she could take back the things she'd said. Perhaps Katherine had needed to hear them, but not that way, she realized, not so abruptly.

Edwina might have liked to escape in her work, but things weren't much better on the job. The attorneys for the Benjamin Braxton estate were disputing her fee, and nothing, not even her boss's impassioned arguments on her behalf, could sway them. What they wanted to give her—a flat fee for her services rather than a percentage of the estate—wouldn't begin to pay off the lien.

At least she could take comfort in Ned Dillinger's pride in her performance. Her boss was impressed that she'd not only found Holt but had intercepted a drug deal at the same time. In a show of support, he offered to send her back out on another assignment immediately, but Edwina wasn't ready for the rigors of a new case. She had a heartful of unfinished business to resolve. "I have some ghosts to bury, Ned," she told him, asking for a week of personal leave. He granted her request without hesitation.

Edwina's unfinished business was the memory of

Diablo's cruelty. His behavior in the motel haunted her. It came back to her in stark flashes that she knew would never be exorcised until she understood what had driven him to it. A deep background check hadn't been necessary in order to locate Chris Holt, but it was Edwina's only recourse now. She knew of no other way to reconstruct his past and unlock the mysteries.

It took the majority of the week and innumerable dead ends before Edwina uncovered a history so dark and disturbing, she didn't want to believe it. Her main source was a society reporter who'd written a series on the Holt-Braxton marriage thirty-odd years before. Edwina found the sixty-two-year-old journalist living in a retirement home in Hartford, and the woman's revelations were shockingly straightforward.

"Somebody squashed the real story," the reporter admitted with evident relish, "squashed it but good. It was years later before even *I* learned the truth, and I followed that family closely. The Holt couple didn't die in a car wreck. Wiley Holt ran his wife down one night in a drunken rage. Seems she was trying to stop him from going out carousing, and it turned into something ugly. Afterward, he crashed the car into a tree and killed himself. Could have been grief, I suppose, or the alcohol."

Edwina quelled the revulsion she felt. "They had a child," she said, meaning Chris Holt. "What happened to him?"

"The boy had only one living relative that anyone knew of—Gillian's brother, Benjamin Braxton the fourth. Braxton packed the kid off to boarding school first thing. Probably didn't know what else to do with him. Cute little guy, he was. About four or five when it happened. Freckle-faced and skinny."

By the time Edwina left that afternoon, she was badly shaken. The woman had painted an alarming picture of Chris Holt's childhood. He'd grown up in boarding schools, the victim of a silent, insidious abuse and neglect. His uncle had provided him with all the material advantages but nothing remotely resembling the love and nurturing a child needed to thrive.

Fortunately the reporter had been able to provide Edwina with a name that had eluded Edwina in her original search for Holt—the woman who'd been the housekeeper the night Chris Holt disappeared at nineteen. The woman proved easy to find but difficult to interview. She was concerned about jeopardizing her current position with a prominent Ridgefield family.

"They had a terrible fight that night," she admitted to Edwina after much prodding. "The young man, Mr. Holt, said he was quitting school—Harvard, I think it was—and Mr. Braxton exploded. He called the boy terrible names, said he was scum, just like his father. Before it was over, he'd told the boy everything—how his father had cheated and gambled and drank, how Wiley Holt had run down his own wife and then killed himself."

"The boy didn't know?" Edwina asked.

"No one knew. Braxton had fixed it with the police, I guess."

"What did Holt do then?"

"He flew out of there in a rage. The old man tried to stop him. He told the boy he had a bad heart. He said they'd lose the family business if the boy didn't finish school and take over."

"And what did Holt do?"

"He told Mr. Morgan to 'rot in hell.' " She tapped her lips nervously. "Those were his exact words, I remember. He said the old man had taken the only thing he had, his memories." She shook her head sadly. "I felt bad for the young man. He left that night and never came back."

Suddenly Edwina understood the depth of Diablo's conflict. It wasn't just anger that drove him; it was guilt. He might even have felt some responsibility for his uncle's death when she told him about it. She'd probed a festering wound. Unknowingly, but that hadn't made it any less painful.

She thanked the woman quickly and left, her head whirling with the implications of what she'd learned. The need to see Diablo again rose in her swiftly. Going to him seemed as natural as breathing. Now that she understood the conflicts that were driving him, she could help him resolve them. Wasn't that what you did when someone you loved was in trouble?

A nervous smiled surfaced as she played back her own thoughts. *Loved?* That was an interesting choice of words.

By the time Edwina pulled into her driveway in Norwalk thirty minutes later, she had talked herself out of anything so rash as catching a plane to California. Even if she could help Diablo, even if she *did* love him, he'd given her no indication that he shared those feelings. Quite the opposite. What he had given her was the bum's rush. He'd as much as said he never wanted to see her again.

"Temporary insanity." She voiced the sobering phrase again as she cut the car's engine and let herself out. She'd been responding instinctively to the pain of his childhood. She'd let down her guard for a second, and all the feelings had come rushing back. Get a grip, Edwina, she thought, *please.*

Despair weighted her steps as she stopped by the mailbox on her way into the house and picked up the usual bills, a catalog or two, a stack of junk mail. She dropped the pile on the kitchen counter as she entered, determined to go through the motions of her daily routine. A quick inspection of the refrigerator revealed a jar of green olives, some leftover pepperoni pizza, and a half-gallon of chocolate milk. It figured, she thought. Beth had supermarket duty that week.

"Eddie?" Edwina was on her way up to her room when she heard her mother's voice.

"Come here, will you?" Katherine called. "I'm in the living room."

Edwina hesitated on the stairs, not sure whether to be pleased or apprehensive. Her mother hadn't stepped out of her bedroom in days. Katherine's reappearances usually signaled that the crisis was past, but Edwina didn't know what to expect in this case. Especially since she was no longer playing the role of protector.

She came upon Katherine reading the newspaper in the alcove's sunny window seat. The room smelled faintly of lavender, and her mother was dressed in a green corduroy skirt and cotton-knit sweater. It was a scene very much like something out of Edwina's childhood. Among her mistier and more pleasant memories, Edwina remembered the many times she'd found her mother hidden away in the alcove reading the Sunday papers. Edwina would curl up next to her and listen in ecstasy while Katherine read the comic strips aloud—*Peanuts, Pogo,* and *Brenda Starr.* Those were the warm years, Edwina thought.

As it was, she had become so used to seeing her mother in a robe or a housedress, she hardly knew what to say. Katherine actually had a hint of color in her cheeks.

"Are you feeling better?" Edwina asked cautiously.

"Yes, dear, I am." Katherine's voice was shaky, but her smile was strong as she handed Edwina a section of the paper. "I thought you might want to see this. It concerns you."

Edwina shook the paper straight and glanced at the article. The first thing that struck her was the headline: "Biker Busted on Drug Charge." The byline was Christopher Holt, *L.A. Times.*

"Christopher Holt?" Edwina's heart raced ahead of her eyes as she skimmed down the column and came upon her own name: "Edwina Moody, an investigator from the East Coast, shadowed the suspicious pair and witnessed the drug transaction. Described as both shrewd and beautiful by an unidentified Warlord gang member, Ms. Moody was also instrumental in apprehending one of the suspects as he tried to flee the scene."

Edwina stopped reading and released a shaking breath. The paper rattled in her hands. "At least he's accurate," she said, trying to cover her feelings with sarcasm. "The beautiful part, I mean."

"He's quite a good writer," Katherine agreed.

Edwina started again, read the entire piece hungrily, and then turned to the article next to it: "Warlords Clean Up Act With Charity Run." The short article described a fundraiser in which the motorcycle gang rode en masse to a children's hospital in Los Angeles to donate toys. There was even a picture of Killer and Food Chain. In the background, Edwina could see Squire, Carmen, and several other gang members she recognized.

Edwina's smile tilted sadly as she stared at the familiar faces. It was odd. She'd been with them only a short time, certainly not long enough to think of them as family or even close friends, and yet a wave of loneliness passed through her. She missed them all. She missed *him*.

She looked up and saw Katherine's eyes on her.

"Did you care about him a great deal?" her mother asked.

Edwina folded the paper in her hands and nodded, too emotional at that moment to trust her own voice.

A quiet fell around them then, as though neither woman knew quite what to say. Katherine finally broke it. "I've been thinking about what you said, Eddie. That business about not languishing . . . and I suspect you're right." She plucked a thread from her skirt. "I have been carrying on these past few years, haven't I? Rather like Camille . . ."

Edwina dropped to her knees beside Katherine. "Mother, I'm sorry about what happened."

"No, it's all right. It really is. I don't imagine I left you much choice."

Edwina caught her mother's hand and squeezed it quickly, a brief and telling awkwardness that ended as the back door slammed shut. Footsteps clattered through the kitchen. The refrigerator door was opened and flung shut. In the next seconds Edwina could hear Beth riffling through the mail. And then a scream rocked the house.

"Look at this!" Beth burst into the room, waving an opened envelope in one hand and clutching a banana in the other. "It's a check, Ed."

"Beth, that's my mail!" Edwina snatched the envelope from Beth's hand, glanced at its return address, and pulled out a check from the Dillinger Agency. It was signed by her boss.

She stared at the zeros with mounting disbelief as Katherine and Beth joined her. The estate attorneys must have come through, Edwina realized, stunned. The check was for the full percentage. It would cover the lien and then some. It might even get Beth started in college and set up a nest egg for Katherine.

Dumbstruck, the three women looked at one another.

Edwina let out a muffled gasp of joy. Beth belted out a "Wow!" And then, like a trio of jubilant teenagers, they all joined hands and screamed.

Moments later they were in the kitchen, toasting their future with chocolate milk. "How about it?" Beth cried. "Do I get to go to the Cosmic Zombies concert now, or what?" Edwina only laughed, but Katherine looked a little overcome by all the excitement.

"Mother"—Edwina automatically assumed the parental role—"maybe you should go up and rest."

"Not on your life." Katherine ticked a finger at both of her girls. "I've been resting for years. I want to knock myself out." She gave Edwina a quick tremulous smile and mouthed the words "thank you."

Edwina nodded, her laughter mingling with the sudden heat of tears. She wanted to hug her mother, but she was afraid it might be more than either of them could handle at the moment. She gave Katherine a thumbs-up instead.

In the meantime Beth was riffling through the rest of the mail. "Get this! Here's another one for you, Ed," she said, handing Edwina a beautiful engraved envelope.

They all went quiet as Edwina opened the envelope and withdrew an orchestra ticket for the opening night of the ballet season at Lincoln Center in Manhattan.

"Who's it from?" Beth demanded.

Edwina pulled a note from the envelope. "It says, 'Congratulations! Enjoy yourself. You deserve it. Love, Ned.' "

"Your boss?" Katherine exclaimed. "What a lovely gesture. It must be his way of saying 'well done.' You're going, of course."

"By myself?" Edwina fingered the invitation and shook her head. "No—no, I'd feel awkward."

Beth smirked. "Wimmpeeee."

Katherine produced a wry smile. "Life goes on, Edwina."

Twelve

Late the next afternoon Edwina began her preparations for a gala night at the ballet. She started with a symbolic act that she hoped would free her from the recent past forever. "Out, damned spot," she mumbled, scrubbing the remnants of Diablo's tattoo from her shoulder as she stood in the jet spray of her shower. It was time to take her own advice and get on with her life.

Her skin was reddened and tender by the time she was done, but she had a bittersweet sense of victory. Bruised but liberated, she thought. Sadder but stronger. Now that she had done everything humanly possible to wash away the painful memories, she could truly start over. His mark was gone. Edwina Moody belonged to no one but herself.

She sanctified the ritual of renewal by choosing a dress she'd never worn before. The strapless sheath had been given to her by a friend who'd gained some weight, and it had been much too sophisticated for the old Edwina Moody.

Pressing the dress to her body, she faced the mirror and was thrilled with the way the glimmering black taffeta complimented the honeyed tones of her skin and her tousled halo of golden hair. She was dazzlingly blond and tanned from so many hours of riding in the summer sunshine.

"This will be an auspicious night," she vowed softly, "A night for fanfare, trumpets—and new beginnings." Edwina had never thought of herself as beautiful, but she did at that moment. She was. Beautiful.

There were other changes, too, she realized, emotional shadings that were more subtle than the obvious physical differences. The woman in the mirror was less innocent in many ways. Her fiery idealism had been tempered by reality. Her eyes held a deeper understanding of the frailties and strengths of human nature, a deeper respect for its amazing resilience. She knew about love now—passionate, transforming love with a man. And she knew more than she wanted to about heartbreak.

It was twilight when Edwina exited her taxi in front of Lincoln Center's steps. She joined the crowd of bejeweled guests advancing upon the Performing Arts Center and was buoyed by the communal feeling of anticipation. It was opening night. The atmosphere was alive with animated chatter, and the excitement was infectious. The very air was electric.

As Edwina ascended the stairs, the plaza's fountain came into view, a jeweled tiara in the falling light. Stopping for a moment to appreciate its beauty, she listened to the water's muted thunder and was reminded of glistening mountain rivers and tumbling waterfalls. Opening night? She touched the satin bodice of her gown and felt a delicate pulse beating beneath her fingers. It was *her* opening night.

Through the silvery music in her head she thought she heard someone saying the word "Princess."

Her breath caught, but she refused to turn or even to look, because she knew she couldn't have heard any such thing. It was wishful thinking. She only *wanted* to hear that word, *that voice.* She continued walking and then hesitated, only to hear it again.

"Princess?"

The fountain roared in her head as she searched the crowd. The pulse she'd felt a second before was beating in every cell of her body. A sea of gowns and tuxedos blurred as she turned in a semicircle . . .

and saw a man across the plaza. Half-shadowed by a colonnade, he was tall, dark, and stunningly familiar in a black tuxedo.

Edwina's eyes recognized him before a storm of conflicting messages reached her brain. Diablo? No, it couldn't be. Her senses collided, trying to sort out the contradictions. There was no motorcycle, no flying dark hair.

All the ways she remembered him strobed through her mind, a heartstopping kaleidoscope of images . . . the outlaw and his fire-breathing motorcycle . . . the pagan, naked in the moonlight, his body streaming with water . . . the wolf with luminous eyes.

She strained to see him. Was this the same man? "Diablo? . . ."

He started toward her, and the fountain's radiance caught the iridescent green of his eyes. He was clean-shaven, but somehow in the play of light and shadow, the contours of his face seemed even more dramatically pared.

"What are you doing here?" She didn't ask the question so much as breathe it.

His mysterious smile held a sparkle of white and tan. "Same thing you are, Princess. Opening night."

He glanced over his shoulder at the center, and she realized his long hair hadn't been cut short, as she'd first thought. It was tied back in a ponytail. Not that it mattered. He was beautiful either way.

When he turned back to her, it was as though he couldn't keep his eyes off her a moment longer. "Black . . . ," he said, appreciating her dress. "It's definitely your color."

"Yours too."

They both laughed, and as the tension eased, Edwina realized that it was really he. Her soft laughter held a shimmer of disbelief. "What are you doing here, in New York?"

He glanced at her hair as though the thought of touching it were preeminent in his mind. "I've got some business."

"Business?"

"Legal business, unfinished business . . . the will."

He'd come back to claim his inheritance? Edwina tried not to show her surprise and elation, but restraint didn't come easy. She wanted to shout with joy. "What made you change your mind?"

"A lot of things," he said, but his eyes held a different message. His eyes said there was only one reason he'd come back.

Bells started ringing all around Edwina, and for a moment she thought it was her imagination. *Bells?* She scanned the area, bewildered, and saw that the crowd had begun filing into the center. The performance was starting.

Somehow they were in their appropriate seats moments later, waiting for the ballet to begin, but Edwina could barely remember how they'd gotten there. She was still dazed by his appearance. She was thunderstruck. It felt like a dream, an impossibly beautiful dream, and she was afraid to breathe for fear that she would wake up.

Her body was bombarding her with signals. It was telling her to laugh and cry and make a perfect fool of herself by tearing her program into confetti. But she didn't do any of those things. Instead, she went very still, her brain beginning to whir as she tried to make some sense out of what had happened. She turned to him after a moment and studied his profile. "*You* sent the invitation?"

His eyes twinkled. "You do like *Swan Lake?*"

"I love *Swan Lake.*"

"Actually I knew that," he said, laughing at her soft astonishment. "Ned told me. Nice guy, your boss."

He took her hand as the curtains parted and the stage went aglow with light. The warmth of his skin next to hers was a catalyst for the physical sensations that Edwina's brain had been blocking. This time her body did respond. In a big way. For several seconds she was pleasantly awash in soft chills and thrills and tiny streamers of light. She felt like a teenager on her first movie date. She felt alive and radiantly female. There were so many things she wanted to know about him, so many questions that had to be asked, but she couldn't formulate any of them. Her mind wouldn't let her think anymore. It would only let her feel.

The performance was already in full swing some moments later when she leaned close to him. "I don't even know what to call you," she whispered.

"What would you like to call me?"

"Chris Holt, I guess. That has a nice ring to it."

He stroked her thumb with his. "Call me whatever you want. I'll come."

Edwina was only half present through the rest of the first act. The music and dancing played exquisitely at the edges of her mind, but they couldn't penetrate. She was suspended in a trancelike awareness of the moment. Her world had spun down to the very air she was breathing and to the man next to her. Everything seemed to be hesitating, even her thought processes. Her heartbeat had slowed to a whisper. As though it were waiting for something, watching to see if Edwina Moody could possibly have everything she wanted. Was she a woman within a stone's throw of her wildest dreams?

"Chris Holt," she murmured at one point, as though accustoming herself to the sound of his name.

At intermission they drank champagne, shared soft private laughter. And got lost in each other's eyes.

He took her empty champagne glass away and held it a moment, touching the warmth where her fingers had been. His gaze turned irresistibly green as he studied her, his smile sexy. "Forgive me, Princess, but you look good enough to eat . . . and I'm feeling a little like the big bad wolf tonight."

Edwina tried to return his smile, but her heart was too erratic. There was no escaping him.

He tilted her chin up. "Your eyes changed when I said that. They darkened. Do you like it when I talk to you like that?"

Like it? Edwina felt a deep clutch of excitement that left her flushed and breathless. It wasn't a question that required an answer, luckily, because she couldn't have managed one if it had. Her body was having trouble remembering elemental things like breathing.

"Do you want to stay for the next act?" he asked.

She must have answered because he took her hand and they exited the center in a headlong rush, descending the steps to a waiting limo. It was dark and intimate inside the limo, and again Edwina could hardly believe what she was doing. Or that she was with him. She had to keep telling herself that it was real.

"A limo?" she said as he signaled the driver to pull out.

His laughter was heavy with irony. "They tell me I'm about to be rich. And you're royalty. I thought we'd go in style tonight."

The city's myriad lights flickered brilliantly past them as they glided through streets teeming with nightlife. Fascinated by all the activity, Edwina surveyed the sights happily. When she'd had her fill, she turned to him and voiced the questions tumbling around in her head. "What are you doing here?" she asked. "What changed your mind about coming back?"

He didn't answer her right away, and as she waited, Edwina realized what she wanted to hear—that he was going crazy without her. Or even that he'd been persuaded by her staunch stand on responsibility.

"Chris?" she said, curious.

He was staring out the window, and Edwina knew a moment of panic as she registered his pensiveness. Harsh lights and shadows streamed over his face, and his eyes seemed fixed on some distant point. "Chris, what's wrong?" She was terrified that he might be distancing himself, shutting her out just as he'd done in the motel.

His shoulders moved with a deep expiration, and then he reached for the black silk tie that ringed his snowy white collar and pulled it loose. "There are a couple of things you should know about me, Ed," he said quietly, turning to her. "It's a messy story. I'd rather not inflict it on anyone, especially you."

"Do you mean your past, the problems with your uncle?"

"Yes—"

Relieved, she stayed him with her hand. "It's all right. I already know."

"You do? . . . How?"

She hesitated as it occurred to her that he might not appreciate what she'd done. He was a private man, and she had no way of knowing if he would understand why she'd had to know who Christopher Holt was. "I took time off to do some research after I got back," she said, praying he wouldn't hate her for violating his privacy.

"Research on me?"

"Yes." She met his eyes, an entreaty in her voice. "You forced me out of your life, and I had to know why. I was hurting." *I was dying*, she thought.

He was silent for so long, she looked away. "You're angry."

"No . . . I'm sorry."

He pulled her into his arms and hugged her, burying his face in her hair. "God, I'm such a belligerent bastard. I ought to be shot for treating you like that."

Edwina closed her eyes, nearly dissolving with relief. His lips were tender and urgent as he feathered her temple with kisses. His long fingers contracted possessively in her hair. He *was* a belligerent bastard, she thought exultantly, but he was *her* belligerent bastard, thank God.

"You never answered my question," she said after a moment, pulling away to look at him. "You did come back for me, didn't you?" The question forced an intimacy that made Edwina's breath catch as she waited for his answer. Luckily he didn't make her wait very long.

"I came back *for* you," he said, "and because of you."

"Oh . . ."

His handsome features blurred as Edwina's eyes suddenly swam with tears. She ducked her head, feeling very foolish and emotional. "You get double bonus points for that one," she said, laughing against the tremor in her voice.

"It's true, Ed." He stroked her hair, unhurried, letting her have her momentary self-consciousness. "You were right about the feud with my uncle being an ancient dispute. It was time I put it to rest. I thought I was free when I walked out of his house fifteen years ago. I wasn't. The past was a hook that embedded itself deeper, the more I fought it. I finally realized that I could never be free until I came back and dealt with it."

"And have you dealt with it?"

"I'm working on it."

"All of it? Even your feelings for your uncle?"

He laughed softly. "I'm working on it."

Edwina was struck by the total lack of animosity in his voice. There was a quality of quiet resignation in the statement and in his manner that made her believe he was much closer to coming to terms with his past than even he might realize. "So, what now?" she asked.

"Now I have my uncle's stock-brokerage firm to contend with, plus his other holdings and a fifty-acre estate in Connecticut."

"Heavy responsibilities."

"Not really. I can handle the portfolio, and I figured Killer might like to get his hands on the brokerage, Braxton Securities."

"Killer? On Wall Street?"

"Why not? The kid's a genius. He'll either make us all fabulously wealthy or bankrupt the entire country. Either way, it should be fun to watch."

Edwina had caught the collective term. "Make 'us' wealthy?"

His smile was suddenly a grin, raffish and irresistible. "Yeah, us. As in me and someone else. That's the other thing I have to do, Ed. Find the right woman, settle down, and have a tribe of kids. I'll never be able to spend all that money by myself."

"*You?* Settle down?" The question came out so spontaneously, she didn't have time to tone it down.

He feigned displeasure. "You sound like you think I'm genetically incapable."

That was the moment that Edwina realized she didn't know whom she was dealing with. The outlaw biker she'd fallen in love with *was* genetically incapable. Diablo had had an unbridled lust for freedom in his blood. Diablo had been untameable. She had loved that about him. And yet this man, Chris Holt, had a quality that Diablo had fought against ferociously. Edwina didn't know how to describe it except with one very inadequate word. *Vulnerability.* There was a hard and beautiful vibrancy deep in Chris Holt's emerald eyes, as though he'd lived through a hellish pain in the last few days and had emerged on the other side of the turmoil, knowing what he wanted. Chris Holt could admit that he needed a woman, she realized. Diablo could never have done that. Diablo couldn't allow himself to need anyone.

"If I'm the right woman," she said, "I think you'd better tell me. Quick."

"Can you rope a pig?"

She laughed as he caught her face in his hands.

"Ed, I love you," he said, his voice wondrously rich and husky. "I'm going to say that to you a lot if you'll let me. I'm going to say it until you believe me."

"I think I do believe you, but say it to me anyway."

He bent to take her lips, and Edwina felt herself sinking into the emerald green of his eyes, drifting in the wondrous heat and strength he gave off, *drowning sweetly in his arms.* He curved a hand to the nape of her neck, deepening the kiss, and she let out a sound that was soft and alarmed.

"Mmmm," he said, whispering against her lips. "I love the noises you make."

"That's me—noisy."

He turned serious then, his eyes intent as they

probed hers. "I'm not trying to press you, Ed, but did I mention the estate in Connecticut? It's a hell of a big place. You could probably round up all the kids and senior citizens in Connecticut and still have space left over."

"What do you mean? My agency? My *day-care* agency?"

"It had better be *your* agency, because the only thing I'm good for is teaching lunatic women how to ride motorcycles." A melting tenderness infused his laughter. "Whatever you want, Princess. Anything you want."

She had successfully forestalled tears several times that night, but he was pushing her endurance to its limits. It was a priceless gift he was offering. She felt as though he'd repaired a favorite broken doll and handed it back to her. As he brought her curled hand to his lips and gently kissed her knuckles, she began to blink furiously, then to cry. No amount of sighing or headshaking could stop the hot flow of tears welling up in her eyes. Her aching heart was too full of joy and simple gratitude.

"Now why did you want to go and do that?" he said, his voice hoarsening as he thumbed a huge tear from her cheek and pulled her into his arms. "There aren't too many situations I can't handle in this world, but this is definitely one of them." A fierceness took him as he held her tightly and buried his face in her hair. "Don't cry, Ed. *Don't*, baby. I ache inside when you cry."

His admission made her cry all the harder, of course, tears that flowed like a river, turning the tip of her nose red and making her voice crumble with emotion. "I can't help it," she said. "This is the most beautiful, incredible moment of my life, and I don't want it ever to end. Do you suppose we could ride around in this limo forever?"

"I've got a better idea. Let's have a whole bunch of moments, one right after the other. Then we'll never have to be afraid when one ends."

Edwina exhaled all the shaking air in her lungs as

he rocked her gently. She buried her face in the warmth of his shoulder, wondering if it could possibly be true. Was she supposed to have her agency *and* him? Was that what Providence had in store for her? She couldn't imagine what she'd done to deserve that much happiness. Not that she was complaining . . .

She resurfaced finally, nestling the back of her head into the curve of his shoulder as they streamed through the neon lights of Broadway and the colorful squalor of Times Square. It was going to be quite an experience getting to know Chris Holt. She could hardly wait to take him home to Mother. A smile broke as she imagined Katherine's reaction: "He seems like a nice boy, dear, but that hair. . . ."

A crazy thought hit Edwina then. What if it had been Diablo she was bringing home! The Moody household would never be the same. She actually felt a little pang of disappointment that the outlaw biker was gone. Beautiful, angry, sexy Diablo. Lord! She was going to miss him.

She needn't have worried.

"Where are we going?" she asked a short time later as the limo pulled into an alley behind a multi-storied hotel and came to a stop.

"Another one of those moments I promised you," he said, opening the limo door. "Wait here."

Edwina watched in confusion as he walked to a dimly lit alcove a few feet away and stripped off his jacket and shirt. Muscles rippled in his shoulders as he untied his long hair and shook it free. His eyes flicked her way briefly as he pulled on a black leather vest and tossed his head, sending his long hair streaming, as she'd seen him do so many times before.

As he turned in the light, she was aware of sinewy arms, breadth of shoulders, and a dark diamond of chest hair. There was only one more detail to complete the transformation. Edwina's heart began to pound as she watched him dig the red bandanna out of his vest pocket and tie it around his head.

His green eyes flashed in the dim lights. His profile shimmered with quick, cold arrogance. He was the outlaw again. The devil. Diablo.

A moment later he was rolling a gleaming motorcycle into the lights. Edwina saw the fiery skull and crossbones emblazoned on the gas tank and smiled. It was his bike. He'd either had it shipped or ridden it across the country. And if she knew Diablo, he'd ridden it.

As he returned to the limo and to her, Edwina realized what he had planned. He was going to abduct her on his bike. He would sweep her away to some tiny dark motel and make love to her—roughly, passionately, without preliminaries. He would take her with all the sweet savagery in him.

He opened the door, black leather gleaming in the moonlight, long hair flying. Edwina's heart jumped painfully as he stared down at her, his eyes drifting over her features, lingering on her mouth. A smile flickered as he held out his hand and asked her the same question he'd posed the day they met.

"Trust me?"

Then it had been a lifetime's prudence and a moment's indecision that had held her back. Now it was her thundering heart. Chris Holt had picked her up in a limo, promised her the world, and asked her to marry him. But it was Diablo who wanted her now.

She took his hand.

THE EDITOR'S CORNER

Next month you have even more wonderful reading to look forward to from LOVESWEPT. We're publishing another four of our most-asked-for books as Silver Signature Editions, which as you know are some of the best romances from our early days! In this group you'll find **ONCE IN A BLUE MOON** (#26) by Billie Green, **SEND NO FLOWERS** (#51) by Sandra Brown, and two interrelated books—**CAPTURE THE RAINBOW** and **TOUCH THE HORIZON** by Iris Johansen. Those of you who haven't had the pleasure of savoring these scrumptious stories are in for one bountiful feast! But do leave room on your reading menu for our six new LOVESWEPTs, because they, too, are gourmet delights!

A new Iris Johansen book is always something to celebrate, and Iris provides you with a real gem next month. **TENDER SAVAGE**, LOVESWEPT #420, is the love story of charismatic revolutionary leader Ricardo Lazaro and daring Lara Clavel. Determined to free the man who saved her brother's life, Lara risks her own life in a desperate plan that takes a passionate turn. Trapped with Ricardo in his cramped jail cell, Lara intends to playact a seduction to fool their jailer—but instead she discovers a savage need to be possessed, body and soul, by her freedom fighter. Lara knew she was putting herself in jeopardy, but she didn't expect the worst danger to be her overwhelming feelings for the rebel leader of the Caribbean island. Iris is a master at developing tension between strong characters, and placing them in a cell together is one sure way to ignite those incendiary sparks. Enjoy **TENDER SAVAGE**, it's vintage Johansen.

Every so often a new writer comes along whose work seems custom-made for LOVESWEPT. We feel Patricia Burroughs is such a writer. Patricia's first LOVESWEPT is **SOME ENCHANTED SEASON**, #421, and in it she offers readers the very best of what you've come to expect in our romances—humor, tender emotion, sparkling dialogue, smoldering sensuality, carefully crafted prose, and characters who tug at your heart. When artist Kevyn Llewellyn spots the man who is the epitome of the warrior-god she has to paint, she can't believe her good fortune. But convincing him to pose for her is another story. Rusty Rivers thinks the lady with the silver-streaked hair is a kook, but he's irresistibly drawn to her nonetheless. An incredible tease, Rusty tells her she can use his body only if he can use hers! Kevyn can't

(continued)

deal with his steamy embraces and fiery kisses, she's always felt so isolated and alone. The last thing she wants in her life is a hunk with a wicked grin. But, of course, Rusty is too much a hero to take no for an answer! This story is appealing on so many levels, you'll be captivated from page one.

If Janet Evanovich weren't such a dedicated writer, I think she could have had a meteoric career as a comedienne. Her books make me laugh until I cry, and **WIFE FOR HIRE**, LOVESWEPT #422, is no exception. Hero Hank Mallone spotted trouble when Maggie Toone sat down and said she'd marry him. But Hank isn't one to run from a challenge, and having Maggie pretend to be his wife in order to improve his reputation seemed like the challenge of a lifetime. His only problem comes when he starts to falling in love with the tempting firecracker of a woman. Maggie never expected her employer to be drop-dead handsome or to be the image of every fantasy she'd ever had. Cupid really turns the tables on these two, and you won't want to miss a single minute of the fun!

Another wonderful writer makes her LOVESWEPT debut this month, and she fits into our lineup with grace and ease. Erica Spindler is a talented lady who has published several books for Silhouette under her own name. Her first LOVESWEPT, #423, is a charmingly fresh story called **RHYME OR REASON.** Heroine Alex Clare is a dreamer with eyes that sparkle like the crystal she wears as a talisman, and Dr. Walker Chadwick Ridgeman thinks he needs to have his head examined for being drawn to the lovely seductress. After all, he's a serious man who believes in what he can see, and Alex believes the most important things in life are those that you can't see or touch but only feel. Caught up in her sensual spell, Walker learns firsthand of the changes a magical love can bring about.

Judy Gill's next three books aren't part of a "series," but they will feature characters whose paths will cross. In **DREAM MAN**, LOVESWEPT #424, heroine Jeanie Leslie first meets Max McKenzie in her dreams. She'd conjured up the dashingly handsome hero as the answer to all her troubled sister's needs. But when he actually walks into her office one day in response to the intriguing ad she'd run, Jeanie knows without a doubt that she could never fix him up with her sister—because she wants him for herself! Max applies for the "Man Wanted" position out of curiosity, but once he sets eyes on Jeanie, he's suddenly compelled to convince

(continued)

her how right they are for each other. While previously neither would admit to wanting a permanent relationship, after they meet they can't seem to think about anything else. But it takes a brush with death to bring these two passionate lovers together forever!

Helen Mittermeyer closes the month with **FROZEN IDOL**, LOVESWEPT #425, the final book in her *Men of Ice* trilogy. If her title doesn't do it, her story will send a thrill down your spine over the romance between untouchable superstar Dolph Wakefield and smart and sexy businesswoman Bedelia Fronsby. Fate intervenes in Dolph's life when Bedelia shows up ten years after she'd vanished without a trace and left him to deal with the deepest feelings he'd ever had for a woman. Now the owner of a company that plans to finance Dolph's next film, Bedelia finds herself succumbing once again to the impossible Viking of a man whose power over her emotions has only strengthened with time. When Dolph learns the true reason she'd left him, he can't help but decide to cherish her always. Once again Helen delivers a story fans are sure to love!

In the upcoming months we will begin several unique promotions which we're certain will be hits with readers. Starting in October and continuing through January, you will be able to accumulate coupons from the backs of our books which you may redeem for special hardcover "Keepsake Editions" of LOVESWEPTs by your favorite authors. Watch for more information on how to save your coupons and where to send them.

Another innovative new feature we're planning to offer is a "900" number readers can use to reach LOVESWEPT by telephone. As soon as the line is set up, we'll let you know the number—until then, keep reading!
Sincerely,

Susann Brailey

Susann Brailey
Editor
LOVESWEPT
Bantam Books
666 Fifth Avenue
New York, NY 10103

FAN OF THE MONTH

Carollyn McCauley

After seeing the Fan of the Month in the backs of LOVESWEPTs, I wished that I'd have a chance to be one. I thought it would never happen. Due to a close friend and the people at LOVESWEPT, I got my wish granted.

I've been a reader of romance novels for twenty years, ever since I finished nursing school.

LOVESWEPTs arrive at the Waldenbooks store I go to around the first week of the month. Starting that week I haunt the store until the LOVESWEPTs are placed on the shelves, then, within two or three days, I've finished reading them and have to wait anxiously for the next month's shipment.

I have a few favorite authors: Iris Johansen, Kay Hooper, Billie Green, Sharon and Tom Curtis, and many more. As far as I'm concerned, the authors that LOVESWEPT chooses are the cream of the crop in romance. I encourage the readers of LOVESWEPT who buy books only by authors they've read before to let themselves go and take a chance on the new authors. They'll find they'll be pleasantly surprised and will never be disappointed. The books are well written, and the unusual and unique plots will capture their attention. From the first book in the line to the current ones, they have all held my attention from page one to the last, causing me to experience a variety of emotions and feelings.

Over the years of reading the different romances available, I've cut back on the amount I purchase due to the cost. LOVESWEPT has maintained such a high standard of quality that I'll always buy all six each month!

OFFICIAL RULES TO
LOVESWEPT'S
DREAM MAKER GIVEAWAY
(See entry card in center of this book)

1. NO PURCHASE NECESSARY. To enter both the sweepstakes and accept the risk-free trial offer, follow the directions published on the insert card in this book. Return your entry on the reply card provided. If you do not wish to take advantage of the risk-free trial offer, but wish to enter the sweepstakes, return the entry card only with the "FREE ENTRY" sticker attached, or send your name and address on a 3x5 card to : Loveswept Sweepstakes, Bantam Books, PO Box 985, Hicksville, NY 11802-9827.

2. To be eligible for the prizes offered, your entry must be received by September 17, 1990. We are not responsible for late, lost or misdirected mail. Winners will be selected on or about October 16, 1990 in a random drawing under the supervision of Marden Kane, Inc., an independent judging organization, and except for those prizes which will be awarded to the first 50 entrants, prizes will be awarded after that date. By entering this sweepstakes, each entrant accepts and agrees to be bound by these rules and the decision of the judges which shall be final and binding. This sweepstakes will be presented in conjunction with various book offers sponsored by Bantam Books under the following titles: Agatha Christie "Mystery Showcase", Louis L'Amour "Great American Getaway", Loveswept "Dreams Can Come True" and Loveswept "Dream Makers". Although the prize options and graphics of this Bantam Books sweepstakes will vary in each of these book offers, the value of each prize level will be approximately the same and prize winners will have the options of selecting any prize offered within the prize level won.

3. Prizes in the Loveswept "Dream Maker" sweepstakes: Grand Prize (1) 14 Day trip to either Hawaii, Europe or the Caribbean. Trip includes round trip air transportation from any major airport in the US and hotel accomodations (approximate retail value $6,000); Bonus Prize (1) $1,000 cash in addition to the trip; Second Prize (1) 27" Color TV (approximate retail value $900).

4. This sweepstakes is open to residents of the US, and Canada (excluding the province of Quebec), who are 18 years of age or older. Employees of Bantam Books, Bantam Doubleday Dell Publishing Group Inc., their affiliates and subsidiaries, Marden Kane Inc. and all other agencies and persons connected with conducting this sweepstakes and their immediate family members are not eligible to enter this sweepstakes. This offer is subject to all applicable laws and regulations and is void in the province of Quebec and wherever prohibited or restricted by law. In order to win a prize, residents of Canada will be required to correctly answer a time-limited arithmetical skill-testing question.

5. Winners will be notified by mail and will be required to execute an affidavit of eligibility and release which must be returned within 14 days of notification or an alternate winner will be selected. Prizes are not transferable. Trip prize must be taken within one year of notification and is subject to airline departure schedules and ticket and accommodation availability. Winner must have a valid passport. No substitution will be made for any prize except as offered. If a prize should be unavailable at sweepstakes end, sponsor reserves the right to substitute a prize of equal or greater value. Winners agree that the sponsor, its affiliates, and their agencies and employees shall not be liable for injury, loss or damage of any kind resulting from an entrant's participation in this offer or from the acceptance or use of the prizes awarded. Odds of winning are dependant upon the number of entries received. Taxes, if any, are the sole responsibility of the winners. Winner's entry and acceptance of any prize offered constitutes permission to use the winner's name, photograph or other likeness for purposes of advertising and promotion on behalf of Bantam Books and Bantam Doubleday Dell Publishing Group Inc. without additional compensation to the winner.

6. For a list of winners (available after 10/16/90), send a self addressed stamped envelope to Bantam Books Winners List, PO Box 704, Sayreville, NJ 08871.

7. The free gifts are available only to entrants who also agree to sample the Loveswept subscription program on the terms described. The sweepstakes prizes offered by affixing the "Free Entry" sticker to the Entry Form are available to all entrants, whether or not an entrant chooses to affix the "Free Books" sticker to the Entry Form.